Love is
a time of enchantment:
in it all days are fair and all fields
green. Youth is blest by it,
old age made benign: the eyes of love see
roses blooming in December,
and sunshine through rain. Verily
is the time of true-love
a time of enchantment — and
Oh! how eager is woman
to be bewitched!

A STRANGER'S KISS

Penniless and alone, Darcy felt indebted to Mike Trent: after all he had saved her life and paid her medical fees. So she felt bound to agree when Mike asked her to marry him: it would allow him to carry on looking after his small nephew, and it would only be for eighteen months. But what Darcy thought would be a strictly business arrangement, was viewed by Mike as something completely different. How was she to get out of this predicament?

SONDRA STANFORD

◆

A
STRANGER'S
KISS

Complete and Unabridged

ULVERSCROFT
Leicester

First published in Great Britain in 1978 by
Mills & Boon Limited
London

First Large Print Edition
published August 1991
by arrangement with
Mills & Boon Limited
London

British Library CIP Data

Stanford, Sondra
A stranger's kiss. — Large print ed. —
Ulverscroft large print series: romance
I. Title
813.54 [F]

ISBN 0–7089–2487–5

Published by
F. A. Thorpe (Publishing) Ltd.
Anstey, Leicestershire
Set by Words & Graphics Ltd.
Anstey, Leicestershire
Printed and bound in Great Britain by
T. J. Press (Padstow) Ltd., Padstow, Cornwall

For Huey, who always believed

1

THE storm that had threatened ever since she set out broke suddenly. A flash of lightning lit up a field on the left of the highway. A loud clap of thunder roared immediately afterwards, and Darcy winced and gripped the steering wheel tightly. Then the rain, which had been only warning drops before, fell with unexpected ferocity.

She switched on the windshield wipers and slackened her speed. The countryside was suddenly a lonely and deserted vastland and she wished fervently that she was sheltered cosily somewhere, anywhere, instead of on her own in the middle of this terrifying display of Mother Nature.

The air grew sharp and cold as the wind whipped up and whistled through the cracks and crevices in the old Volkswagen. This was a late winter norther. Yesterday had been warm and sunny, the sort of day Texas advertised to lure tourists. March was the most unpredictable month of the year, never able quite to make up its mind what it wanted to do, always just hovering between winter and spring. Darcy shivered and switched on the heater. The thin pale blue sweater she wore wasn't adequate and her coat was packed away in the boot.

Another flash of lightning zigzagged brilliantly across the sky in front of her, lingering, it seemed to Darcy, for an interminable time before it faded away at last. She chewed her bottom lip nervously. Her every nerve now was tautly strung with fear. The rain was so heavy she could scarcely see a yard in front of her. She slowed the car to a crawl and leaned forward tensely, straining to see the yellow dividing line in the centre of the road.

A sudden gust of wind took the car broadside and, for a terrifying instant, it shimmied and shook uncontrollably. Darcy's knuckles whitened around the wheel as she struggled to keep the car on the road.

No traffic met her coming from the opposite direction. She peered anxiously through the window. If she could only see a farm house she would stop and ask if she could stay until the storm passed over, but there were no houses, only endless fields and highway, telephone poles and a few billboard signs advertising bread or motels in Houston and other points south. It was as if she was all alone in this storm-tossed world.

The sky was dark now — almost like night, although it was just ten-thirty in the morning. The rain on the windshield was a solid sheet and the wipers were completely ineffective. The car hit a patch of backed-up water, which sprayed against the side of the car, and suddenly a dog loomed up from nowhere, darting across the highway directly into her path.

Automatically Darcy slammed on her brakes. The car slithered drunkenly, and horrified, as another gust of the strong north wind slammed into the car, she felt the car flipping in the air, and closed her eyes, awaiting the inevitable.

When she came to, she was lying in a puddle of water. The torrent of rain was brutally assaulting her face, stinging her eyes. Despite all this, she saw two things before her — a raging fire and a giant of a man. But how could a fire burn in all this rain? she wondered fuzzily.

The giant bent down beside her and touched her hand. She was aware of dark, intense eyes, a straight nose, a hard jawline. He seemed to be pulling something over her body, and glancing down she saw that it was a black raincoat. She lifted her eyes to his face again. His mouth was hard, drawn into a grim line; his face was colourless. And then, incredibly, the lips softened as he leaned over and brushed her lips gently with his. Then the giant blurred as she floated away again, away from consciousness and pain.

When next she awoke she was aware that her head throbbed painfully and her neck felt stiff. Her entire body felt sluggish and heavy. She lay perfectly still, apathetic, eyes closed. It seemed such an effort to attempt to open them.

But after a few moments she roused herself and her eyelids fluttered up. The room she was in was dimly lit. Without moving, she lay gazing before her as her eyes gradually became adjusted to the darkness. There was a faintly antiseptic odour in the air. She made out the shape of a television set mounted near the ceiling in the corner opposite the bed. Beside the bed, on her left, was a counter and wash basin. Beyond, was a wide door, partially closed. The bed itself had rails. A rack stood beside the bed with an inverted bottle. Incredulously, Darcy realised her arm was strapped to a board and a needle was plastered to her vein.

Her brows contracted slightly. She must be in a hospital. What was wrong with her? Panic seized her for an instant and then remembrance flooded back — the storm, the dog, the accident! She had had a car accident. There had been a fire and a giant of a man with unreadable dark eyes who had knelt beside her and touched her cold, wet lips with his warm ones.

But how ridiculous! The face she pictured in her mind was the face of a stranger and why would a stranger kiss her? No, that must be some hallucination — probably a result of the drugs that must surely have been administered to her.

She closed her eyes again wearily and tried to think back over what had happened clearly and rationally. She had been driving to Houston and it was raining — that much, surely, she had not imagined. But thought made her head ache worse. She stirred restlessly and this brought pain to both her legs.

At once she was aware of someone standing beside her bed, someone gripping her free wrist. She opened her eyes again to see a grey-haired nurse gazing at her watch as she took Darcy's pulse.

When she had finished she smiled warmly. "Ah — and how are you feeling, love?"

"My head hurts," Darcy admitted.

"Well, of course it does," the nurse agreed. "You've been through quite a lot." She patted Darcy's arm in a motherly fashion. "Now, just relax. I'm going to call the doctor and tell him you're awake and then I'll bring you something for that head." She smiled again and went briskly from the room.

For the next few days Darcy slept a great deal, her mind in a state of fuzziness. But one morning she awoke just at daybreak. The ever-present throbbing in her head was gone at last. Her wide-set blue-green eyes held a spark of alert interest in life once again. She glanced out the window. The sky was midnight blue, streaked with pink and orange. Darcy sucked in her breath in pure enjoyment. She lay perfectly still, completely engrossed in the spectacular panorama.

The sky was bright gold threaded with red when she finally turned away. It had been years, when she'd been a child, since she had last seen so beautiful a sunrise. She moved slightly and had a view of the room now and suddenly her heart hammered crazily.

Seated in the chair next to the bed was the giant. His eyes were closed and a large-brimmed Western hat rested on one knee. Darcy studied him for a long moment and then suddenly he opened his eyes and they met hers directly. There was a stern, forbidding look on his face until he saw her. Then he smiled. "Good morning."

"G-good morning," she stammered nervously. Had he kissed her, she wondered wildly, or had her subconscious simply dreamed him up, dreamed up his kiss? Perhaps even now he wasn't real.

He rose slowly from the chair and looked down at her from his considerable height. His tall, sinewy body looked vibrantly real and alive, hard and lean and browned by outdoor living. She had time to notice that his dark hair was touched with grey at the temples. It leant him a distinguished air, along with thick eyebrows, a straight, strong nose, a firm upper lip and a fuller, sensuous lower lip. She guessed his age to be somewhere in the vicinity of the middle thirties.

"You're looking much better," he said as he studied her almost dispassionately. "You're not so pale today." She didn't answer. She could only stare at him, uneasily aware that he had obviously been observing her a good deal while she had been totally oblivious to her surroundings. It made her feel suddenly shy and her face warmed with embarrassment.

"I'd better ring for a nurse," he said abruptly. He pressed the buzzer, then moved towards the door. When the nurse came in, he smiled once more. "Your patient seems wide awake this morning."

The nurse was young and attractive with her dark hair making a foil against the white of her uniform. She smiled at the stranger before even glancing at Darcy. "That's good news. Now, if you'll just step outside, sir?"

He passed through the door without

8

glancing back once at Darcy. The nurse approached the bed. She looked at Darcy with professional assessment and then nodded and smiled. "You do look much better. How do you feel, Miss Mills?"

"Fine," Darcy answered disinterestedly as the nurse began to check her blood pressure. "Who is that man who was here?"

"Why, don't you know?" the nurse asked in surprise. "That was Mr Trent — the man who saved your life." She smiled. "If you had to have an accident you couldn't have picked a better man to get you out of it!"

"I didn't pick him," Darcy said drily.

The nurse looked at her, startled. "No, I guess you didn't, exactly, did you?" She laughed. She wrote something on a chart, then shook a thermometer.

Darcy asked, "How long have I been here?"

The nurse popped the thermometer into Darcy's mouth. "A week," she answered.

Darcy jerked the thermometer out and demanded incredulously, "A week? That — that's impossible! What's wrong with me, anyway? When can I leave?"

The nurse's eyebrows puckered in a worried frown. "Now, don't go getting yourself upset, Miss Mills. You'll have me in hot water. The doctor will be in later this morning and then he'll be able to answer all your questions."

Darcy protested, but now the nurse was evasive and cautious. "You just relax," she suggested soothingly. "That'll get you well quicker than all this fretting." She bustled away, leaving Darcy alone with her anxious thoughts.

And they were frightening ones. The first and foremost worry was how she was going to pay for all this hospital care without any insurance to cover her. She glanced around in agitation. The room was a private one and must be the most expensive of all. Why hadn't they placed her in a ward? And next, what was she going to do once she left the hospital, as she must do at once? She was supposed to have started her job as a sales clerk in a dress shop in Houston five days ago. Now, not only had she no means of paying for all this hospital care, but she had no means of a livelihood when she got out either. She was sure the job would not have been held for her after she didn't show up. Now she would have to start the wearying chore of job-hunting all over again — and what would she live on in the meantime? Had what little money and clothes she had in the car been saved for her? She would have to ask. All her possessions in this world had been in the boot of her Volkswagen.

She was feverish with impatience by the time the doctor came at nine. He was a grey-haired man in his sixties and he came forward to her bed immediately and patted her hand in a fatherly fashion. "Hello there, little miss. I understand you're fretting the nurses — that must mean you're on the mend." He smiled at her and the skin crinkled at the edges of his eyes. "I'm Dr Jordon, by the way."

Darcy moved her head in agitation. "When can I leave here, Dr Jordon? I must leave soon. I don't have the money for — all this." She swept her hand in an arc. "I don't have any insurance to pay for it."

Dr Jordon pulled up a chair and sat down beside the bed with the air of a man who had all day to chat. "Don't worry your head over that, my dear. It's all being taken

11

care of. All you need to do is concentrate on getting strong and well."

"Taken care of?" Darcy asked, puzzled. "How can it be? This is a private room and . . . "

Dr Jordon cut in. "Mr Trent tells me you saw him when you woke up this morning." He eyed her keenly as he paused for a moment, then he added, "He's paying your expenses, Miss Mills."

"Mr Trent?" she asked in a daze. "But — but why? The nurse told me he was the man who saved my life when I had the accident, but . . . "

"That he did," Dr Jordon said approvingly. "You were trapped beneath the car. Michael Trent happened along and saw it and he pulled you free — just in time, too, the car burst into flames moments later. I'm afraid all your belongings burned too, but what does that matter? You wouldn't be here to talk about it all if it hadn't been for Trent."

Darcy's eyes were large with wonder. "I — I have a great deal to thank him for, then, haven't I?"

Dr Jordon nodded. "You certainly do. He's been very concerned about you. You've

12

had a severe concussion and for the first three days and nights he sat with you hour after hour because we couldn't find a private nurse. Later we had Nurse Lovell for the nights, but last night she was ill herself and couldn't come. That's how you came to find Trent here with you this morning."

Darcy's throat felt parched and dry. "Why should he have done all this — for me — a stranger?"

The doctor smiled and shook his head. "I can't answer that for you, my dear," he said gently. "Trent seems a very generous man, but for all that he's very close-mouthed about his motives. You'll have to ask him that for yourself." He stood up. "You're a lucky young woman," he said. "You've had a severe concussion, as I said, but you seem out of the woods now. Outside of a few cuts and bruises, mainly on your legs, you're fine. And the legs will heal without leaving any scars. Now, I'm going to order you a soft diet for a day or two and see how you go on. You've been on glucose for a week, so perhaps a bit of broth and gelatine will be welcome. And I'll look in on you again tomorrow morning."

"Yes," Darcy said absently. "Thank you, Doctor. Oh, by the way, where am I?"

"Where are you?" He looked confused for a moment. "Oh, I see. This is Austin." He nodded pleasantly and went out.

Darcy slept in restless fits most of the rest of the day. Obligingly, she tried to swallow a bit of broth and juices that were brought to her, aware that the sooner she regained her strength, the sooner she could leave the hospital.

During her wakeful periods she wondered when the man named Michael Trent would return. She felt an urgent need to thank him — for saving her life and for seeing to financial matters for her stay at the hospital. She felt a need, too, to assure him that just as soon as she was able, she would pay him back the money he had expended on her behalf. She didn't know how or when that would be possible, but it would have to be done.

Bleakly, she stared at the wall, wondering how she was going to go on, wondering what was to become of her. A lone tear trickled down her face and, impatient and

14

ashamed, she brushed it away roughly. Never before had she indulged in self-pity, though it would have been easy to do so many times, and she was not going to start now.

2

MICHAEL TRENT did not return that day after all and Darcy wondered why he had apparently been so conscientious about her before. For some reason it disappointed her, and as a result she did not sleep well that night.

The next morning the same nurse who had attended her the morning before came in and dumped several packages on to the foot of the bed. She smiled cheerfully. "Good morning. I brought you a few necessities."

"Necessities?" Darcy struggled to sit up in bed and look alert.

"Nightgowns, a toothbrush, robe and slippers and of course, a hairbrush, comb, lipstick and powder."

"But – but – how?" Darcy spluttered. "The doctor said my handbag burned with the car. I have no money to . . ."

"Tut, tut," laughed the nurse. She drew out a soft pink nightgown and held it up for approval. "Mr Trent gave me the money yesterday and asked me to get what you needed."

Darcy's face flamed scarlet at the thought of Michael Trent buying her nightgowns. "I can't — " she began. "I can't possibly accept them!" Embarrassment spread through her.

The young nurse frowned at her. "And I thought you'd love it," she said stroking the silky nightgown. "Besides, you can't go on wearing those horrid green hospital gowns, now can you?"

Darcy looked down at the offending coarse linen gown she wore and her lips trembled. It was true it was humiliating to have to wear such an abomination all the time, but how much more humiliating to accept such intensely personal items as that from a stranger — a man. The nurse seemed to read her thoughts. "Take them, honey. You need them and you're in no position to be choosy who does the giving. Besides, he'll probably never know the difference. I understand he went back home last night."

"Home? He — you mean he doesn't live here?"

"No, worse luck. He's a rancher. His place is some distance from here, I think."

17

She sighed. "Now if he lived here, I might have had a chance to get him interested in me. I don't meet many men as attractive as he is around this place. Usually it's the ugly old men you find hanging around the hospital — or the cute, young besotted new fathers." She groaned, and Darcy laughed in spite of herself.

The nurse nodded as if satisfied, pulled three other gowns from the box and displayed them. "Come on, Miss Mills, pick one out for today. If I don't hurry and get out on the floor soon, the head nurse will be axing for me!"

Darcy finally allowed herself to be coaxed into slipping on a soft yellow gown and then the nurse helped her brush her hair and apply a light coat of lipstick. "There," she said approvingly. "You look great. I'll bet you even feel better."

Darcy admitted it. The silky texture of the gown felt luxurious against her skin after the rough hospital gown and it was wonderful to feel her hair soft and neat again. "I feel human again," she said, "but I still don't think I ought to have accepted all this."

The nurse gave her a reproving look.

"The man obviously has money to burn," she stated emphatically. "You should have seen the bundle he handed me." At the flush stealing over Darcy's face and throat, she chided, "Come out of the Dark Ages, honey. Nowadays girls think nothing of accepting personal things from a man they're not married to. I can assure you if I was in your place I'd just smile prettily at him and thank him very nicely next time he comes." She grimaced and added, "But you see how it is with me. *I'm* the type men give money to in order to buy things for other girls!"

Darcy laughed in spite of her self-conscious worries at the disgusted expression on the nurse's face. Then with a wave, she was gone, and Darcy was left to her sobering thoughts.

For the next five days, Darcy expected her benefactor to appear, and as a result she was in a constant state of nervous agitation. But hanging more heavily on her mind was the problem of money. Each day she remained in the hospital built higher an already horrifying medical bill. She had no money behind her; no job, no money to live on once she got out.

On Sunday morning it rained again, the first time since the day of Darcy's accident. "Foul day," observed Dr Jordon when he came in for his daily visit.

Darcy nodded. "You're early today," she said.

He smiled grimly. "My family had planned a picnic outing for today."

Darcy smiled in sympathy. "I'm afraid you're in for a disappointment. Looks like it's set in for the day."

Dr Jordon sat down in the chair next to her bed. "My grandsons will be the most upset. They don't believe in nice, quiet Sunday afternoons at home." He smiled, dismissing his family problems and looked keenly at the girl in the bed. "How are you today?"

Darcy shrugged. "All right."

"Headaches?"

She nodded. "Not so bad as before, though." Suddenly eager, she leaned forward. "I'm much better, actually, Doctor. When can I leave here?"

He held up a hand. "Don't rush things, my dear. I want you one hundred per cent well when I let you go. I've a feeling you're one of those people who never sit around twiddling their thumbs as a rule."

He was right, of course. But then never before in Darcy's twenty-two years had she ever had the time, or a reason, to be idle. After the doctor left her, Darcy stared bleakly out of the window. Rivulets of glittering raindrops ran down the window panes. Beyond, the grounds soaked in the rain while the still bare branches on the trees dangled sparkling diamond droplets of water.

She considered how much her life had changed for her recently — all so incredibly fast. Her father had died when she was just fifteen. He had been an electrical repairman for an appliance store in the small panhandle town where they had lived, and after he died she and her mother had lived on his pension and social security.

Darcy's mother had never been in good health, so her going to work was out of the question. But because of her ever-increasing medical bills and their reduced income, it was not long before they had had to give up the comfortable home where they lived and taken instead a small rented cottage.

Her mother had resented this lowering of her standard of living and, along with her ill-health, she grew ill-tempered as well. Darcy did her best to placate her constant grievances and by the time she was seventeen, she handled virtually all the domestic chores in the house, before and after going to school each day.

After her husband's death, Mrs Mills didn't encourage visitors, and because of her heavy duties at home Darcy had an almost non-existent social life. In her senior year in high school, one or two boys in her class showed an interest in her and asked her for dates, but in each instance, when the boy had come to her house, Mrs Mills had been so rude that she effectively killed any further interest the boy might have had in her daughter. After the second time, Darcy had been so humiliated that she had never tried again.

After her graduation from high school, Darcy had contemplated finding a job in town. Going to college had been out of the question — there was no money for that. But when she broached the subject of a job, her mother had complained bitterly. She was in bad health and she needed someone in constant attendance. How could her only daughter be so callous as to want to leave her completely alone all the time?

For the first time in her life Darcy had wanted to rebel, but in her heart she knew she never would. Because for all her whining, complaining ways, her mother truly was ill — her doctor had made that bluntly plain to Darcy.

And so for the past four years she had lived a narrow constricted life at home. As the years went by, her mother's health deteriorated rapidly until, for the past year and a half, she had been a totally bedridden invalid. It had taken all Darcy's strength and mind to cope with the full-time care her mother required. There had been no time at all for self-pity or for daydreams of might-have-beens. Girls she had gone to school with either married and began families or went away to large cities to start careers while Darcy stayed at home, and as through a fog, watched her youth slipping away from her. But as there was nothing she could do about it, she had resolutely refused to dwell on it.

But a month ago the end had come

abruptly, without warning. She had gone into her mother's room with her breakfast tray, just as she did every morning. But there was no complaint this morning of a sleepless, pain-filled night. Instead, the face on the pillow looked almost serene in its stillness, and for that reason alone Darcy had been grateful. At last her mother was free of pain.

It was several days later that the realisation came that she also, in a different way, was free, and two weeks later, once all the legal chores were out of her way, she had driven to Houston to look for a job. As long as she was beginning a new life alone, she had wanted to make a complete break with the unhappiness of her past.

And she had been lucky. On her second day in Houston she had found a job as a sales clerk in a small, exclusive dress shop. True, the pay was low, but considering she had had no job experience behind her, Darcy had felt herself extremely fortunate. She had returned home only long enough to go through the personal effects in the house. She gave her mother's things to a local church for their charity bazaar and then she had loaded her own things into the Volkswagen. How excited she had been that morning! And now, instead of working at a new job, instead of setting up a new life for herself in an apartment, she was here in a hospital, worrying frantically how she would ever get out from under such a heavy debt.

Footsteps sounded on the tiled floor, jerking Darcy back to the present. She turned her head from the window, expecting one of the nurses. But advancing towards the bed was the tall stranger. "Good morning," he said in a deep voice. "My name is Mike Trent."

Darcy's throat suddenly constricted nervously. "Yes," she whispered weakly, "I — I know."

There was a small silence as they looked at one another. He was so absurdly big, Darcy thought fleetingly. A giant. The bright glare of the overhead light made his tanned face look darker than before. Today his Stetson and boots were gone, and he now wore a neat blue casual suit with a white turtleneck pullover shirt. "May I sit down?"

Darcy felt her face grow warm. "Of — of course. Forgive me."

He lowered himself into the chair next to the bed and then his eyes studied her again. "How are you feeling now?"

"Much better." She paused, then rushed on, "They told me it was you who saved my life, Mr Trent. I — I can never thank you adequately."

"So don't try," he cut in with a bored tone to his voice, which made her face grow pinker. "Listen — I traced your car licence to the town where you lived and I tried to locate your relatives. But the few people there who seemed to know you said they didn't know if you had any family or not."

"No." She shook her head slightly. "I have no family now. My — my mother died only a month ago."

"So I was told. I'm sorry. But if you'll tell me now of any friends I can contact . . . ?"

She shook her head again. "There's no one." And a small, forlorn note crept into her voice, unawares.

"Well, where were you going? Where do you live now?"

"I was on my way to Houston." Somehow the words just tumbled out and it was a relief to talk about it all. "Dr Jordon

26

won't listen to me when I try to talk about leaving," she added in some exasperation. "He doesn't seem to understand how badly I need to get on my feet, to find another job."

"That's because he knows there's no point in discussing it until you're physically fit again."

"But the bills!" She blurted out anxiously. "He said *you* were paying them, but I can't allow that. And in any case, why should you?"

Mike Trent leaned back in his chair, and his eyes half closed as though he were bored again. "I shouldn't worry about all that yet if I were you. Just concentrate on getting well."

"But I *have* to worry about it!" she said irritably. For heaven's sake, he was just as bad as Dr Jordon! Neither of them wanted her to face reality. Did they take her for a child? "It's my responsibility, not yours. And why should you be doing all this for me, anyway? I'm just a stranger to you."

He shrugged his broad shoulders carelessly. "Oh, just call it a whim of mine, I guess."

"A very generous whim," Darcy said pointedly. "Don't think I'm not grateful,

Mr Trent, because I — ”

"Are they feeding you well here?" he broke in abruptly. "You look mighty thin to me, and you're still too white. Maybe I could smuggle you in a hamburger and malt or something."

Darcy stared at him for a long moment as though he'd gone crazy. Then suddenly she laughed and her eyes twinkled. "How very subtle, Mr Trent. Why are you so averse to being thanked properly for your generosity?" she asked curiously.

He grinned now too, and she was suddenly conscious of how strong and virile he looked. "Let's just say it's a bore and leave it at that."

"Then you shouldn't go around saving people's lives and helping them out financially into the bargain," she said in a tart voice that lifted his eyebrows. "Well, I won't thank you any more if it annoys you — ”

"Good."

"But," she went on, ignoring his interruption, "I intend to pay you back every cent somehow some day. I — I just wanted you to know that I — that I'm no sponge."

"I never thought you were," he said languidly. "But you're not to worry about that money, you understand? If you want to pay me back, well and good, but don't think there's any rush about it. You take care of yourself first."

She looked at him for a long moment. "You're a funny man," she said at last. "You're so very kind and yet you don't want anyone to acknowledge it."

His face darkened and he stood up and towered over her bed. "I've never been accused of being kind or generous before," he said. "In fact, I've been told by some who should know that I'm cruel and selfish."

Darcy stood her ground despite his anger and shook her head. "I don't believe a word of it," she said flatly.

"No?" There was a curious light in his eyes. He took a step closer to the bed and his eyes strayed from her face to her slender neck, to her white, silky throat, to the swell where her breasts rose. "You're very lovely," he said in a soft, sensuous voice, "in that thin green nightgown. And you're so small — light as feather, I bet. If I wanted to — er — impose my will on you, you'd be helpless to stop me."

He leaned over her, putting his hands on the bed on each side of her. Her face scorching, her eyes large as saucers, Darcy jerked the bed covers up to her throat. "You — you wouldn't dare," she sputtered. "Good God this — this is a *hospital*! The nurses . . . "

He straightened back up again and his eyes were mocking. "Ah, yes, the nurses. But you see my point, Miss Mills? I'm not a kind man — or a very generous one."

"Go away," she said in a choking voice. "Please go away."

He nodded curtly. "Right." With a casual wave of his hand, he added, "Take care." Then he was gone.

3

THE next week dragged by painfully slowly for Darcy. The weather improved and by Wednesday she was being wheeled outside in a chair to sit on a tropical patio. She had plenty of time to think of the man to whom she owed so much — Michael Trent. He was an intriguing, perplexing man. He had been so generous, so kind to her, and then angered by her gratitude he had deliberately set out to make her dislike him. Was he afraid she was about to fall in love with him and expect him to take care of her from now on? If that was the case, he hardly needed to worry.

She smiled grimly to herself. Her natural strong spirit was returning along with her health and now she thought with wry amusement that if she had not still been so ill, so weak that day, he would not have got away with intimidating her. If it happened today, for instance, she would bluntly tell him to behave himself or she'd ring for a nurse and have him thrown out, gratitude or no.

Oh well, it was past. They had parted with antagonism, deliberately provoked on his part, and Darcy suspected that Michael Trent had left her life for good as abruptly as he had entered it. Which was just as well. She really wasn't up to sparring often with a man like Michael Trent. Now that he'd completed what he'd considered his duty to her, she was not likely ever to see him again. All the same, some day soon, when she had a job and was earning a salary, she would begin paying him back the money she owed him, bit by bit. But for saving her life she could pay him nothing, not even thanks. He had made that plain enough.

But the first order of business was to get a job. As soon as she had been well enough, she had written to the owner of the dress shop in Houston who had hired her. A tiny frown creased her brow now. That lady had written back, consoling with Darcy over her unfortunate accident but making it abundantly plain that because Darcy had not turned up, she had had to hire another girl in her stead, and that for the foreseeable future there would be no further openings in her shop. Darcy had confided in the young nurse who had befriended her, Carolyn Lane, and she had promised to keep her ears open around town and see if there were any jobs available in Austin. Now Darcy did not feel particular about where she lived at all, so long as she could work and support herself. But she knew it would not be easy. She had virtually no experience to back her up and these days a lot of people with college degrees and years of work experience were begging for jobs. It was a depressing thought.

On Friday morning Darcy sat in the armchair in her room beside the window and studied the situations vacant ads in the newspaper. Dr Jordon had told her that if she kept improving in the way she had been doing, he would dismiss her from the hospital at the end of next week. With pen in hand, she was circling any ads that sounded promising with the idea of telephoning and arranging interviews for the moment she was released.

Carolyn Lane breezed into the room and sang out, "See what you have, you lucky girl?"

Darcy stared, wide-eyed, as the nurse set a bouquet of long-stemmed red roses on the window ledge. "But — but who?" she sputtered.

The nurse removed a small white envelope from the bouquet and handed it to Darcy with a smile. "Some secret admirer, I bet. Wish I could stay and drool with you, but I'm swamped." She rushed from the room and slowly, almost reluctantly, Darcy opened the envelope and drew out the card.

There was just one word — '*Forgive?*' and '*Mike*' was signed at the bottom with a bold, dark flourish.

Darcy chewed her bottom lip. Now why? She could see no particular reason why Michael Trent should bother to apologise to her. After all, what he had done he had done deliberately. Why indeed had he ever taken any interest in her beyond saving her life, anyway? It was curious. She read the note again. There was no mention at all of whether he would attempt to visit her again.

Strange man! With a puzzled smile, she tucked the card away in a drawer and then went to the window and inhaled the lovely perfume of the roses.

By Sunday she was feeling almost completely herself again. She had done away with the wheelchair and when Dr Jordon came for his morning visit, she was sitting in the bright sunshine of the tropical patio, chatting with an elderly woman patient.

When she looked up and saw him, she smiled gaily. "Good morning, Doctor. I hope your family is planning another picnic outing today?"

He laughed and sat down beside her. The elderly woman murmured something and went indoors. "Yes, indeed, Miss Mills. My grandsons refused to take 'no' for an answer today."

Darcy looked up at the bright sky. "I don't blame them," she said wistfully. "It's a perfect day for a picnic."

He did not stay long. When he was gone, Darcy stayed on in the patio alone, reluctant to return to the confines of her room. Now that her release was so near, a new problem loomed ahead. She had virtually no clothes to wear when she left the hospital. It was an embarrassing problem. Darcy sighed. She supposed she would have to appeal to Carolyn Lane for help. Perhaps Carolyn would lend her enough money to purchase one or two street outfits. But she hated to ask. She knew that nurses didn't earn enormous salaries and it might create a hardship for her. But the only other person she felt she could ask for a loan was Dr Jordon, and her face flushed at the idea of having to ask that kindly gentleman for clothes money. Still, what choice was there? Clothes she would have to have, no matter what the source.

She stood up to go indoors and, head bent, began to move. Suddenly she was stopped short by running into something solid, and she lifted her head and gasped. "Good morning," Michael Trent greeted her. His hands had shot out at impact and now they gripped her arms. He looked down at her from his great height and observed, "You're a tiny thing, aren't you? I'd forgotten just *how* small you were."

Darcy swelled indignantly to her full five feet one inch height and glared at him. "Just because you happen to be a giant," she snapped, "there's no reason to go around looking down on other people!"

"Bristly too," he mused.

She tried to back away, but his hands still gripped her. "Peanut," he said with the air of having given the matter great thought. "That's what you are, a little peanut."

"I don't have to stand here and listen to you call me names!" she sputtered angrily.

"You do, you know," he said. "Besides, I have something important to talk to you about."

"Well, maybe I don't want to talk to you."

His eyebrows lifted. "What? Is that any way to thank the man who saved your life?"

This time it was Darcy's eyebrows that lifted. "I distinctly remember that you said being thanked was a bore. But if you want to go through the process again I — "

"I don't," he cut in rudely. "That was just to shut you up, only it doesn't seem to have worked." He held her arm. "Come on, Peanut, let's sit down. It's a beautiful day and we should enjoy the sun. The other times we met it was raining."

"I've already enjoyed the sun," she pointed out obstinately.

"So enjoy some more." He released her arm and sat down on one of the benches and stretched out his long legs. When she didn't move, he looked up at her with a curious look on his face. "I don't bite," he said.

Not at all reassured, Darcy reluctantly sat down beside him and settled the long flowing blue robe around her.

For a long moment silence stretched out between them. The only sound was the tinkle of water cascading down in the stone fountain. When the silence showed signs of continuing indefinitely, Darcy looked up at last from her clenched hands and met his eyes, which were intent on her. "Well?" she demanded impatiently. "What did you want to talk to me about, Mr Trent?"

"Mike," he said. "Call me Mike." He was watching her closely as he went on slowly, "I came to ask you to marry me."

Darcy stared at him incredulously and then shook her head. "It's as I suspected," she said solemnly. "You're stark, staring mad!"

Mike Trent threw back his head and laughed. "You do have a way with words all right, Peanut. Now, do you want to hear my reasons for asking, or do you want to call the men in the little white coats?"

Darcy smiled. "That's what I ought to do," she admitted. "You've got to be crazy, of course. But maybe I ought to hear you out first. Then I can give the doctors all the evidence they need to lock you away from other innocent people."

He grinned without comment, then leaning back against the bench, he stretched his arm along the length of it behind her, but not touching her. "It's this way, Peanut. I need a babysitter and a housekeeper and you need a job. I thought maybe we could work out a deal. The marriage would be a temporary one only."

This time she looked at him fully in the face and saw that he was serious. "Go on," she said quietly.

"Well, my brother's wife died a little over a year ago. My brother was all cut up about it, of course."

"Of course." Darcy didn't even realise she spoke.

His eyes flickered over her face briefly and he went on, "Their baby, Kenny, was only a year old at the time. Don brought him to the ranch for my housekeeper to look after six months ago, then he went out to the Persian Gulf to work. He's an engineer with an oil company. He asked to go." Mike shifted his position a little and Darcy was aware of his hand lightly touching her back, but he seemed not to notice it, intent on what he was saying. "Well, I can't blame Don — he badly needed to get away. But it meant I have the care of Kenny for two years, still have a year and a half to go."

"But if you already have someone caring for the child, where do I fit in?"

"Emily is getting too old to have full-time care of an active two-year-old. She's in her sixties and I can tell you, Kenny's a handful. She'll stay of course, as long as I need her, but she really wants to retire and move to Oklahoma to live with her sister. She was just about to go when Don asked me to take Kenny and I persuaded her to stay. But it's hard on her, and I promised her I'd try to find someone else to take over so she can go."

"And you want me?"

He looked down at her and now he smiled almost gently. "Well, I remembered you'd said all you'd ever done was care for your mother and your home. A two-year-old is a very different proposition from an

40

invalid adult, of course, but you're young and I figured you'd be able to cope with him better than Emily. Too, you wouldn't have all the housework and cooking to do. One of my Mexican hands' wife helps Emily in the house every day."

"Then why not let her care for the child?"

He shook his head. "It wouldn't work. Maria is a very good, willing worker and she adores Kenny, but she speaks only broken English. Felix made a trip to Mexico and brought her back with him last year. She's learning English pretty fast, really, but I can't let her have the sole care of the baby. He's just at the stage where he's learning to talk. It has to be someone else to care for him."

Darcy nodded. "All right, I can understand your reasons for needing someone," she said, "but were you serious about marriage? I mean, I can't see why that's necessary if I'm merely going to work for you."

He grinned at her and a flush stole from her throat up to her face as his eyes roamed over her tiny but well built figure.

"Believe me, Peanut," he drawled, "it

would be necessary. My ranch is rather remote, but not uncivilised. There are neighbouring ranchers who would take a dim view of a beautiful young woman living alone in the house with me, if you exclude Kenny. And somehow I don't believe my neighbours would accept him as an adequate chaperone."

Her face stung with redness. "If I'm just an employee, surely they would soon accept that."

He shook his head. "Don't bet on it. Country folk still have pretty strong moral convictions, despite what goes on in the cities nowadays. But there are other reasons, too, why if you take this on a marriage is necessary. I've got several young, single ranch hands who live in the bunkhouse. They don't get into town and see pretty girls very often and when they do they sometimes get a little carried away. I don't want to spend my time bailing you out of difficulties with my men. But if you come as my wife they'll know it's hands off and you'll be treated with kid gloves."

"Yes," she said slowly, "I suppose I see what you mean." She looked down at her hands that were twisting nervously in her lap. Shell pink fingernails dug sharply into soft skin. "Then it would be strictly a business arrangement — a temporary one?"

"Yes. The duration to be only until Don returns to claim his son. But the marriage would have to appear real to others — I'd want no talk on that score. So far I've only explained to you what I need. Now let's talk about the benefits in it for you."

"F-for me?" she looked up in confusion.

Mike laughed almost harshly now. "Of course. It's a business deal, isn't it? I'm a fairly rich man, Peanut. But before you agree I must be honest and tell you that I live very simply. I'm a hard-working rancher. My house is large and comfortable, but it's not — not — "

"Ostentatious?" she ventured, peeping up at him.

"That's right. And as I explained, you'd be needed to work — not just sit around looking pretty like a lot of rich men's wives do. Though Maria does most of the housework, you'd still have a lot to do yourself, especially, as I said, caring for Kenny. But you would have your fair share of free time — I wouldn't expect you to devote Kenny twenty-four hours a day. Maria can relieve you any time you want. As my wife you'll have all the money you might reasonably want to spend, and once the marriage is ended, we'd not only count your debt to me cancelled, but I'd see to it that you had an adequate income for life so that you'd never need to worry about another job."

She shook her head now and jumped to her feet angrily. "You *do* take me for a sponge!" Her blue-green eyes had darkened threateningly like a stormy sea.

He stared at her calmly. "What on earth are you talking about?"

"I mean the lifetime guarantee you're dangling in front of me," she all but hissed. "My word, man, you saved my life, you've paid my hospital bills, now you're offering me the chance to be your wife — a business arrangement, to be sure, but still with all the advantages that go with it. Isn't that enough payment for a year and a half or so of work? There's a word for the type of woman I'd be if I took more from you beyond that, and believe me, I have no intention of ever being called it!"

Again he startled her by throwing back

his head and laughing. Since Darcy could see no humour in it, she glared furiously at him. Mike reached out a hand and pulled her back down beside him. Then he leaned forward and brushed a finger gently across her cheek. "You never fail to surprise me, Peanut. I apologise humbly if I've insulted you."

"Well, you did," she said stiffly, with a sullen look still on her face.

He looked at her curiously, almost as though he was examining her like some weird species of insect life beneath a microscope. "I wonder how many other women would have considered it so," he said softly. "You look most attractive when you're so righteously indignant. Did you know that?" When she did not answer, he asked in a different tone of voice, "Well, what is it to be?"

"Oh, I'll do it, of course," she said irritably. "You know what sort of tight fix I'm in."

"Now that's not a very gracious acceptance to the only marriage proposal I've ever made," he replied.

She looked up and met his gaze. "Oh, I know it," she said crossly. Then a smile tugged at her lips. "You — you just made me furious, that's all. But of course I'm really deeply grateful to you and — "

"No gratitude," he said harshly, suddenly blazingly angry. "It's a mutually profitable business deal . . . There's no reason for any of your blasted gratitude at all."

This time Darcy laughed. "All right, I'll keep it to myself. But at least let me say I'll try my best not to fail you."

His eyes flickered enigmatically. "You won't," he said with calm assurance. He leaned forward and brushed her lips gently with his, so gently she might almost have imagined it. He said, "Just to seal our bargain."

4

THREE weeks had passed since the day Mike Trent had made his incredible proposal. Now, as Darcy sat at the dressing table in Carolyn Lane's bedroom, brushing her hair into a silvery cloud around her small face, Carolyn said, "I'm going to miss you, Darcy. Are you sure you want to go through with this? It's not too late to back out yet, you know."

Darcy stood up, laughing, and hugged her new friend briefly. "If I remember right, the first time we met you were carrying on about how attractive he was and how you wished he lived here so *you* could get his attention."

Carolyn grinned, unabashed. "So I did. But I'm more his size, I could handle him better. You look like a midget beside him. You'll never be able to hold your own with a man like Mike Trent."

Darcy smiled. "Oh, I think I can manage." She glanced at the clock next to the bed. "Look at the time, Carolyn! We'd better finish dressing." She turned back to the mirror and picked up her lipstick, hoping the doubts in her heart didn't show on her face. It wouldn't do to let Carolyn realise how nervous and uncertain she felt. As far as Carolyn was concerned, she was supposed to be marrying for love, a storybook ending come true. She had no idea it was all just a cold business arrangement, and a temporary one at that. Yet through all her apprehensions Darcy knew that even had she not been in any financial difficulties at all, she would have agreed to marry Mike anyway. It was the only way she could repay him for saving her life, though she could just hear his angry tirade if he knew. A tiny smile of amusement touched her lips at the thought.

Carolyn looked around the room. "Are you all finished packing, Darcy?"

"Yes, I think so. I finished while you were in the shower." She glanced around too, her eyes searching for anything forgotten. For the past two weeks, ever since her release from the hospital, she had stayed, at Carolyn's insistence and Mike's approval, in her apartment. It had been a busy two weeks, shopping for clothes, going for fittings, visiting the hairdressers'. Only yesterday she had paid her final check-up visit to Dr Jordon. He had pronounced her fit at last and had expressed pleasure over her upcoming marriage. "I'll confess I was worried about you, young lady," he told her. "But I know Trent will take good care of you — he's done that already. I'm sure you'll have a wonderful life ahead of you both."

Darcy had felt a fraud listening to him, just as she felt a fraud with Carolyn. It hurt her to trick her closest friends, but Mike had made it plain that no one was to know the truth, and to be honest, her own pride held her silent as well. She was no more eager than he to let others know what a fake this marriage was.

Now Carolyn came from the closet carrying the dress Darcy would wear for her wedding in just one hour's time. She slipped it on and stood solemnly regarding herself in the mirror as Carolyn did up the tiny buttons in the back. It was a soft eggshell white lace dress with a simple, scooped neckline, slim, long sleeves, and a short skirt that swirled lightly against her legs. She knew that she looked nicer than she ever had in her entire life before, and she sighed softly with regret that it could not be for a man she loved, a man who loved her. This was not at all how she had always imagined herself on her wedding day.

Carolyn hugged her briefly. "You look beautiful, Darcy. Your Mike will really be impressed after seeing you so pale and wan in the hospital for so long. I do hope you'll be happy." The doorbell rang and Darcy was spared any comment as Carolyn exclaimed, "That must be the florist."

She returned a moment later, not with a florist's box, as she had expected, but with a small, elongated jeweller's box. Darcy took it hesitantly and opened it slowly. Inside was a beautiful string of perfectly matched pearls. "Oh, Darcy!" Carolyn gasped. "It must have cost him a fortune. And after that fabulous engagement ring, too!"

Darcy looked down at the lovely oval-shaped diamond on her left hand and shook her head wordlessly. Considering it was a mere temporary marriage, Mike was going rather overboard in his efforts to convince the world that it was the real thing. She lifted the pearls and took out the card that came with them. '*The groom's gift to the bride. I hope you'll wear them. Mike.*'

Wear them? Of course she would. They were so lovely. She clasped them around her neck as Carolyn again went to answer the door. But her thoughts were not happy as she regarded their lustre next to her throat. They were just one more tangible bit of evidence of Mike's generosity — just one more thing to have to leave behind with Mike once the marriage ended. And already she knew that when the time came it would be hard. It would not be the giving up of rings or pearls which would be difficult, but the doing without Mike's gruff, generous kindness.

Suddenly she shook herself mentally. She had been ill and weak so long that she had begun to lean on Mike completely. It had been too easy to let him barge in and take over her life and arrange everything for her. But that had to stop. Now, it was her turn to help him — and she would, and when the time came to say goodbye she would do it with no regrets. She studied her pale face critically and applied a dab more of colour to her cheeks. Then she smiled and was glad to see a sparkle to her eyes. This was her wedding day. Maybe she was not marrying for the usual reasons, but that did not mean she had to look as though she was going to a funeral. Whatever happened from now on, she wasn't going to let Mike down.

The wedding was a simple one in a private parlour of a hotel. When Darcy first entered the room with Carolyn, for a moment everything swam blurringly before her eyes. Pure panic suddenly seized her and she actually took one step backwards, as though to escape. But then Mike was beside her, touching her hand gently, and everything came back into focus.

He looked very handsome in a dark suit with a subdued gold and white striped tie. But his face looked as pale as her own must be. This thing must be as difficult for him, she thought, as it was for her. Curiously, she had never thought about his side of it before. He smiled suddenly and then a warm expression came into his eyes. "You look beautiful," he whispered.

"Th-thank you." Her mouth was dry and it was difficult to speak.

"Reverend Stewart is waiting," he added. "Are you ready?"

Jerkily, she nodded and, with her hand still clasped in his, he led her forward.

She had a fuzzy impression of a tall potted palm in a corner of the room, of soft beige draperies to the right, of a small, thin minister, but ever afterwards she would never be able to describe the room or the minister. She was aware of one thing only — of Mike at her side and the vows they exchanged.

When it came her turn to pledge her vows, she felt herself a fraud and a liar as she shakily whispered the words " . . . in sickness and in health, from this day forward, until death us do part." Why, she wondered desperately, could they not have left that part out?

Then she felt Mike's hand tighten on her own, as though he was aware of her qualms. Gravely, she watched as he placed his ring upon her finger. And then the minister was saying, "I now pronounce you man and wife." It was too late now for escape.

Mike bent and lightly brushed her lips with his. And then they were accepting congratulations from the minister, from Carolyn, Darcy's only attendant and a man named Joe Morgan, who was Mike's best man.

Carolyn and Joe shared an elaborate luncheon with them afterwards. Joe seemed a nice, friendly, outgoing man, a bit younger than Mike, and he immediately paid Carolyn several extravagant compliments, which, to Darcy's secret amusement, were pleasing her friend quite a lot.

Mike's face had been closed and unreadable during the ceremony, but now he was smiling easily as though he was indeed a happy bridegroom. "How are you feeling, darling?" he asked as he placed a glass of champagne in Darcy's hand. "Not tired out, are you?"

The 'darling' jolted her, until she realised it was for Carolyn's and Joe's benefit. So they were to play the game to the hilt, were they?

She smiled brilliantly at him. "I feel wonderful, sweetheart. This is the happiest day of my life."

Mike's dark eyes narrowed at that and Darcy could read a gleam of surprised amusement in them. "And I'm the luckiest man in the world," he said in a low, sensuous voice.

Darcy sought frantically for a retort to this charade, but Joe spared her. "Okay, lovebirds," he protested, laughing. "That's enough. We're still here, you know!"

Mike grinned. "So you are. Have some champagne, Carolyn?"

By the time the luncheon was over and Darcy had changed into a suit dress of lime green linen and joined Mike in his maroon Buick for the four-hour drive to his ranch, she *was* tired. It had been an enormous effort to keep up the gay pretence of happily wedded bliss. And the knowledge that the pretence was just beginning shook her confidence.

Mike glanced at her with sharp concern, noting the pallor in her cheeks beneath the make-up. "I tried to keep it all as simple as possible, but it still wore you out, didn't it?"

She summoned up a smile for him. "I'll be all right." When he looked doubtful, she added, "Really, I will now. I guess I was just — nervous."

"You certainly never showed it, Peanut," he grinned. "You looked as cool as ice."

She smiled with amusement. The only time Mike had ever called her Darcy was during the wedding ceremony. "I'm surprised," she said tartly, "that you didn't say, 'I take thee, Peanut, to be my lawful . . . '"

His sudden laughter broke off her words. "If I hadn't been repeating what the minister said, I probably would have," he admitted.

Darcy nestled back against the car seat. They were on the outskirts of town now headed south. Headed home. I'm Mrs Michael Trent now, she told herself unbelievingly. Her gaze fell on her left hand, where a plain gold band had joined the diamond. She touched her throat and said, "Mike, I haven't thanked you yet for the pearls. They're beautiful."

He smiled at her warmly, which did something just a little crazy to her heart. "Just a little trinket I thought you might like," he said.

"I do like them," she assured him, "very much. Just as I like my ring. But," now she turned on the seat where she could see his finely chiselled profile more clearly, "please don't buy me any more expensive things,

Mike. I feel — beholden to you enough as it is."

He shot her an angry glance. "You're not to feel beholden to me in the least, is that clear? You're my wife now. You're entitled to whatever I can afford to give you."

"That's not so!" she protested. "This isn't — isn't a real marriage — it's a purely business situation. And I can't keep taking such things from you. It isn't right."

"You felt no qualms about letting me buy your clothes," he said in a hard, brittle tone.

"Yes, I did," Darcy said in a cracked voice. "But you know I had no choice." Her lips quivered, and suddenly he relented.

In a softer tone, he said, "Okay, I shouldn't have said that, it was rotten. But listen, Peanut, if I choose to make my wife a gift of jewellery, that's my business. You shouldn't be so rude as to turn it down." In a lighter tone, he added, "Think how you'd hurt my feelings."

"You don't have any feelings to hurt," she returned hotly. Then, with a shrug, she added, "Oh, I give up. You don't even want to be reasonable."

He patted her hand. "Not when it doesn't

57

get me my way," he said.

Darcy felt certain that Mike Trent nearly always got his way about things. He was too forceful, too domineering, for it to be otherwise. She glanced out the window at the countryside flying past. It was a very different day from the last time she had set out on a journey. Then, it had been storming. Today, there was bright sunshine. The trees were putting on their new spring finery, vivid, bright green leaves that dazzled in the light. Darcy could see a farmer in a field of dust as he rode a tractor; they passed a farmhouse, where a woman hung her washing on the line while a small child played at her feet.

"Tell me about your home," she said suddenly, turning her attention back to the man beside her.

"Your home now."

"Temporarily," she returned dryly.

She saw his quick frown, as though he had not liked that, and she wondered why. After all, he was the one who had originated this business arrangement between them, not herself. "Well," he said now, "what do you want to know?"

She spread out her hands, fan-like. "Everything."

He laughed shortly. "That's a tall order! Hmmm, let me see — well, first, the name of my ranch is the Triple T."

"The Triple T," she said consideringly. "That has a nice ring to it. How'd you happen to name it that?"

Mike grinned and Darcy noticed for the first time the tiny laugh lines that crinkled up around his eyes. Those lines added, rather than detracted, from his good looks. "I didn't name it," he explained. "My grandfather did. He was a tall man — I kind of take after him in that respect."

"I've noticed."

His grin was engaging. "Anyway," he continued, "he was also called Tex, so the Triple T naturally came into being. Tall Tex Trent."

Darcy laughed, feeling suddenly light-hearted for the first time since her mother had died. "I love it," she told him. She was silent a moment, then asked, "Are there any near neighbours?"

"If by near, you mean near, no. A few miles away, yes. You'll meet them. Ranch living can be lonely and isolated, but we're not completely cut off. We get together for dinners and visits fairly often."

"And to town?"

"Wilson City is forty-five miles away — about fifteen thousand population. That's where we do all our major shopping. I generally go about once a week, but you'll have the car at your disposal, so you can go more often if you like."

"Thank you. But isn't there any place nearer?"

Mike chuckled. "Venture is only twelve miles away. Population about three hundred if you include all the dogs and cats and chickens."

Darcy's lips curved. "The big city, in fact."

"Just that. It's got a gas station, a small grocery, two churches, three bars, one café and a post office."

"What?" She raised her eyebrows. "No hairdresser?"

Mike shook his head. "You know, I never thought to enquire — remiss of me. Would you have turned me down flat if you'd known there wasn't?"

"Of course," she assured him. "Can you doubt it?" With something of a shock, she realised that she was actually *enjoying* being with Mike. For the first time since she had known him she didn't feel tense and nervous.

After a while she asked, "Is your ranch near Padre Island?"

He shook his head. "We're about seventy-five or eighty miles from Corpus Christi. Have you ever been to the Gulf?"

"No. But I've always longed to," she admitted.

"Then I'll take you some time."

It was nearly five when Mike pointed to a highway marker. "Eighty-five miles to Wilson City, forty from home. We'll be there in an hour."

An hour. Darcy fell silent and with each mile the powerful automobile ate up, she became more nervous until soon she actually dreaded arriving. What had she let herself in for? Taking over the domestic chores did not worry her. Her mother had been particular about how things were done, and Darcy knew herself to be a good housekeeper; a good cook, too. She had always enjoyed cooking. She was not nervous about the baby, either. She had not had much experience with children, but she had always been fond of them and she felt she was as capable of caring for a two-year-old as the next person. No, it was Mike himself who worried her. True, he had been easy and friendly today on their drive, but she had an uneasy feeling he would not be exactly easy to live with. His personality was too arrogant and strong. And the idea of meeting his friends and his neighbours terrified her. How on earth was she going to pull this thing off — pretending to them that their marriage was a real one? Eighteen long months of it. What had she been thinking of to agree to such a mad scheme? Surely if she had appealed to Carolyn Lane or Dr Jordon, they could have helped her resolve her difficulties without her having to resort to such a drastic measure as marriage to a man she didn't love and scarcely knew — a man who wanted her on a business basis only.

But it was too late for a change of heart now. She was out in the middle of a lonely bit of countryside with only her stranger husband for company. Mike pointed to her side of the road. "When you see a fence division, that's where my ranch begins."

It was wide open range except for a few live oak trees and mesquite brush. A few cattle grazed some distance from the road. "What kind of cattle do you raise?" Darcy asked.

"I run Brahmans, Angus and Santa Gertrudis. See that red heifer nearest the fence? It's a Santa Gertrudis."

"Weren't they developed on the King Ranch?"

Mike looked at her approvingly. "Go to the head of the class. They're a cross between the Brahman and the Shorthorn."

A little farther on she spotted several oil pumps bobbing up and down like giant black birds. Mike had oil money behind him, too. Fleetingly she wondered what it felt like to have all the money one needed — no, more than that — enough for all that one wanted. She thought of the financial struggle she and her mother had always had, and shook her head, slightly dazed. She would never get used to money — not even with eighteen months of it.

The car left the smooth highway for a black top farm-to-market road. Then a few miles on it left that too, for a gravelled, rural road that was so narrow it was wide enough for only one way traffic. Darcy hoped they did not meet anyone coming from the opposite direction.

A quail fluttered past overhead and a roadrunner darted across the road, and Darcy laughed. "He looks exactly like the one in the cartoons you see at the movies."

"They're funny to watch, all right," Mike said, and suddenly pointed. "Look quick and you'll see a doe!"

Her eyes followed the direction he was pointing and she watched the deer as it stood solemnly eyeing them. Then, with a graceful bound, it vanished into the underbrush.

A few minutes later the car crossed a cattle guard beneath a swinging sign that proclaimed this was the Triple T Ranch. The gravel road wove between fenced pastures. Mesquite and prickly pear grew in abundance along the fence line. The road curved and, without warning, the house came into view.

The late afternoon sun burnished the windows into copper plates set within the red brick. The house was one storey only, but sprawling. A huge old live oak stood with stately bearing in the front lawn. Beyond it, bordering the house, were shrubs, and at one corner, a bougainvillaea climbed a trellis.

Mike shot her a quizzical glance as he brought the Buick to a stop in the circular drive. "Well?"

Darcy sucked in her breath and turned to smile at him. "It's very beautiful," she said. "Why didn't you tell me?"

He grinned. "I thought it was better to let you decide for yourself." He opened the car door and got out, stretched to loosen muscles cramped by the long drive, then came around to open hers. "I'll get your bags later."

Mike opened the carved front door and Darcy stepped into a large entrance hall. The floor was terrazzo, the walls covered with flocked gold and white design. A very old dark wood library table was against one wall.

"We're home!" she heard him shout suddenly from behind her.

A moment later an elderly woman with snowy white hair emerged from somewhere in the back of the house. A dark-haired, beautiful Mexican girl followed close behind her.

Mike's arm came around Darcy's shoulder and she was drawn close against his chest. She shivered at the unexpected touch and hoped he didn't notice. "Emily, Maria, I want you both to meet my wife."

Emily's faded blue eyes were friendly and she smiled and clasped Darcy's hands. "My dear, welcome to your home."

Darcy smiled. "Thank you Emily. I've heard a lot of nice things about you."

Emily turned slightly and beckoned the Mexican girl who hung back shyly. "Maria, come and meet Mrs Trent."

The girl came forward, a bashful smile on her lips, eyes downcast. Her hair was midnight black, long and plaited and twisted about her head. Her skin was a soft, delicate brown and her lashes were long and alluring. She couldn't have been more than eighteen, Darcy thought. "Am pleesed to meet you, Miz Trent," she said in slow, halting English.

"My husband tells me you are from Mexico," Darcy said. "It's a country I've always longed to see. Perhaps some time you'll tell me about your home?"

Maria lifted her shy eyes and a slow smile stretched her lips. "*Si*, ma'am. If you want, I will be pleesed to tell you about my country."

"Have you got Mrs Trent's room ready for her, Emily?" Mike asked now. "She's just recently out of the hospital and . . ."

"Oh, my gracious me!" Emily exclaimed. "You dear child! I was forgetting that. But never mind, we have your room all ready. Let's get you to bed at once! You must be exhausted!"

"I feel fine, really," Darcy protested. She looked at Mike for help, but he merely shook his head and grinned. "I'll bring in the luggage."

Giving in, Darcy allowed Emily to lead her to her room. It was almost at the end of a long hallway. Emily threw open the door and Darcy stepped inside.

"The bath is over here," Emily said as she opened another door. "The closet is there." She waved a hand to the opposite wall.

Mike came in with Darcy's luggage. Discreetly, Emily excused herself and went out, while Mike stood looking around critically. The carpeting was gold, the furnishings white. The bedspread was a dark blue while the draperies were what Darcy privately considered to be a ghastly blue and pink-flowered design. "When I first built this house," said Mike, "Emily chose the decorations after I'd bought the furniture." He smiled wryly. "I suspect she didn't know much about how to go about it, and I don't know enough myself to change it. But I hope you'll feel perfectly free to change anything in the house you don't like."

"Are — are you sure?" she asked warily, eyeing the draperies.

"Perfectly. This is your home now. Maybe after you've been here a few days you can make out a list of things you want for a start and then I'll take you into Wilson City to look for them."

Darcy nodded. "All right. Do you want me to meet little Kenny now?"

His dark eyes. studied her frankly. "Not now, I think. You look tired. Get some rest, Peanut. Plenty of time to meet Kenny tomorrow."

By this time Darcy did feel exhausted. When Mike left, she took a shower and then slipping on a white nightgown, crawled between the cool, fresh sheets. *I'll just doze until it's time to dress for dinner,* she told herself.

She awakened abruptly to find Mike looking down at her. Dazed, she noticed he had changed from the dark suit he had worn for their wedding into a charcoal leisure suit. "Wake up, sleepyhead," he said, smiling down at her. "You missed dinner."

"Missed dinner?" She sat upright in bed, forgetting the sheer, lacy gown she wore which emphasised her slender throat, her swelling breasts. "I'm sorry! I slept longer than I intended."

Mike sat down on the edge of the bed and took one of her small, dainty hands into his. "Don't worry about it. I knew you needed the rest — it's been a big day for you. Emily will bring you a tray when you're ready."

"Oh, but that's so much bother," she began agitatedly.

"Not in the least," he contradicted. A light flashed in his dark eyes and his gaze roamed from her face to her throat, to the little hollow between her breasts. "You're very delectable-looking in

69

that gown. White, too. In honour of our wedding night?"

One of the gown straps had slid provocatively down over her arm, and Darcy snatched it up again as a slow blush stained her face. "Mike, don't — tease," she stammered. "You know I — we . . ."

His lips on hers stopped the halting words. It was a long kiss. Mike took his time over it as his arms went around her, pulling her soft, warm body against the hardness of his.

The aroma of his shaving lotion drifted up to her. His lips were warm, his touch caressing. Darcy's senses reeled, whirled and completely deserted her, as a quiver of answering desire flooded through her. His lips moved down to her throat, and then to the hollow between her breasts, and Darcy had a sensation of liquid fire racing through her veins. But all at once rationality returned, and she pushed him away. "No!" she said sharply.

His eyes were unfathomable and he looked at her. "No?"

She shook her head and attempted to pull the covers over her with trembling hands. "No. You — have no right! Our marriage is a business arrangement. You have no right!"

Mike released her and stood up, his eyes mocking now as he smiled down at her with grim amusement. His eyes flickered with a dangerous light. "Don't act so naïve, Peanut. Marriage is marriage. I made no promise to you that I wouldn't claim a husband's privileges. And I have a perfect right to make love to my own wife!"

Darcy's face paled and her eyes were large with fright. She jerked the bedcovers up to her chin. "You beast!" she hissed out. "You wouldn't dare!"

Mike's laugh was harsh, almost bitter. "Wouldn't I?" he demanded. "I told you once, Peanut, that I was neither kind nor generous. I was telling the truth."

He turned abruptly and went to the door. With his hand on the knob, he said over his shoulder, "I'll send Emily in with your tray." Then, in the old, mocking voice again, "Sweet dreams, Peanut."

5

D ARCY came awake slowly and, for a befuddled instant, wondered where she was. Remembrance flooded back quickly, however. She was married — married, unbelievable word and she was at the Triple T Ranch. A vision of the scene last night with Mike rose up to haunt her, and a soft red stole into her cheeks. She put up a hand and touched her warm face. Had he merely been taunting her, she wondered, or had he really meant what he had said? She had been apprehensive about his returning to her later during the night, but he had not come. Had she angered him? she wondered.

I don't care if I did, she told herself firmly as she thrust her feet from beneath the warm covers to the carpeted floor. He had had no right to try to make love to her, despite what he had said. The marriage had been a purely business arrangement and she intended to keep him perfectly aware of that fact. Privileges, indeed! If he'd wanted a wife in the real sense of the word, then he just should have looked elsewhere, instead of trying to trick her.

Not that it should have been difficult for him to have found a more willing bride, her thoughts trooped on as she dressed in a cream-coloured skirt and a pale blue blouse. There was no denying that Mike was an extremely attractive man. Nearly any girl he chose to favour with his attentions would have been flattered and thrilled. Surely he could have found a wife in the ordinary way if he had wanted? But he had chosen her, and now he would just have to live with the consequences of his own actions. And on a business footing they would stay — she was quite definite about that.

She thought of the way he had held her, kissed her last night, and now she squirmed with embarrassment. She had not been totally indifferent to him herself, despite her stern resolve. And therein lay the danger. Mike was a magnetic, virile man who would be easy for any girl to fall for, especially one so inexperienced with men as herself. But he had made it plain to her from the start that this marriage was only temporary. Darcy had no intention of going away at the end of it with anything less than a whole heart. She was not such a weak fool as to allow herself to care for a man like Mike Trent.

Fortified by such wise thoughts so early in the morning, she set out down the hall in search of the kitchen.

She found Emily there, seated at the table. A young child, in a high chair, was beside her and Emily was cajoling him into eating his breakfast. Maria was beside the stove and she smiled shyly when she saw Darcy.

"Good morning," Darcy said cheerfully as she pulled out a chair and sat down beside Emily. "So this is Kenny. Hi, fellow," she said, smiling at him.

He was adorable, chubby, with pale blond hair and large blue eyes. He stared at her for a long moment, and then, apparently deciding she was harmless, he grinned at her, showing a few small, pearly teeth. Darcy was delighted.

"Did you sleep well, Mrs Trent?" Emily asked.

"Marvellously," Darcy told her. "I'm

74

sorry I slept through dinner last night. I made extra work for you."

"Nonsense," Emily said stoutly. "You needed all that rest. Are you hungry now?"

Darcy's eyes twinkled. "Starving!" she confided.

Emily smiled, satisfied. "We'll soon get some flesh back on your bones. Maria?"

Maria nodded. "I'll have Miz Trent's breakfast ready in only a moment."

"Has Mr Trent eaten yet?" Darcy asked now.

"Oh, laws, yes, two hours ago," Emily answered. "But he told us not to waken you."

Darcy was annoyed. "I wish you had. If I'm going to be a ranch wife, I'm going to have to learn to get up early, too . . . "

Emily nodded approvingly. "Of course you will. But just now you're still recuperating and need your rest."

"No, I'm tired of being coddled, Emily. The only way I'll get really strong again is by pitching in and getting back to work. I've been idle long enough."

After breakfast, Darcy picked Kenny up from his chair. He held out his little arms willingly and she hugged him to her. "You're a darling, you know that?"

"Dat," he tried to parrot.

She put him down on the floor and took his hand. "Outsite?" he asked hopefully.

Darcy laughed and ruffled his hair. "Okay, fellow. Outside it is!"

It was a bright, sunny spring morning, though the air was still sharp. Darcy was glad she'd slipped on a sweater and pulled one on Kenny too. They walked across the lawn, which was still wet with glistening dewdrops. At the back of the lawn were a few widely-spaced oleander bushes.

A little distance behind the oleanders were several buildings which Darcy could see clearly. Kenny tugged Darcy's hand, obviously wanting to go in that direction. Since Darcy did not see any signs of life, she decided it would be all right to take a look around as long as they were not getting into anybody's way.

One building was obviously the barn, with its stalls and bales of hay. Behind it was a corral. A beautiful black horse behind the fence whinnied at them, and Kenny laughed delightedly. "Hoss," he said, pointing a chubby finger.

Darcy smiled at him, then looked back at the magnificent animal. "I suppose it's a quarter horse," she thought, realising just how lacking her education was when it came to ranches and their animals. The horse neighed at them and pranced around the pen, as though putting on a performance for its audience.

After a few moments they walked over to one of the buildings. It held trucks and tractors and horse trailers. A man was bent over, peering at the motor of one of the trucks.

"Trucks," Kenny told Darcy importantly. "Me like trucks."

The man straightened up and nodded. "Good morning, Mrs Trent. I am Felix Gonzales. Can I help you?"

"No thanks. Kenny is taking me on a tour, as you see. But I didn't mean to disturb your work."

"That's all right," Felix's brown face broke into a grin. "Kenny doesn't have the least qualms about it, do you, old man?"

Kenny grinned as though he understood, and then he led Darcy away again. This time they headed back towards the house, passing by a ploughed vegetable garden. A

77

few young plants were up and Darcy once again felt hopelessly ignorant. Her mother had never raised a garden, so now she had no idea what type of vegetables she was looking at because the plants were still so young. Shrugging, she decided to ask Emily to fill in the gaps of her education before she left, and to explain to her how to prepare the vegetables for the big freezer she had seen in the utility room next to the kitchen. She knew she would never have the nerve to ask Mike about such simple domestic matters. She could just picture the derisive lift of his eyebrows.

For the next two hours she played with Kenny in the yard area just behind the house. He had a sand-pit, and Darcy climbed into it and sat down as though playing in sand-pits was an every day occurrence with her. Kenny squealed with laughter a great deal, and filled pail after pail of sand and poured it in front of Darcy until he finally had a huge mound. Darcy busied herself building a castle which Kenny much admired. "Pretty," he said repeatedly. "Me like."

When he finally tired of the sand, she sat on the patio and watched him ride his tricycle, thinking sadly about the young mother who must have loved him so dearly, yet was unable to watch him grow up to manhood.

Presently they went indoors again and Darcy gave Kenny a bath, amid much squealing and laughing and splashing on his part. Then she took a shower herself to wash away the sand.

The rest of the morning was spent looking over the house with Emily. It was a large, comfortable house, Darcy discovered, without being so large as to be unmanageable. There were five bedrooms, a large, formal living and dining area, a pleasant, panelled family room with a fireplace, and also a book-lined study, where, Emily told her, Mike worked on his accounts.

"I hope," Darcy said, "that you aren't planning to leave me too soon, Emily." The sudden thought of being left alone with Mike, and the care of his nephew and his home, seemed overwhelming.

Emily patted her hand. "I'll stay just long enough for you to be familiar with everything, my dear, and then I'll have to leave. I've had the running of this place so long I'd be a thorn in your side if I stayed longer. You'll be wanting to change things to suit yourself. That's only natural and right for a new bride, but I'm too old to change my ways and that's a fact."

Darcy laughed and shook her head protestingly. "Oh, I'm sure we'd get along, Emily. Besides, I don't know anything about raising a small boy, or what my — my husband likes to eat — or anything!" Her voice ended on a rather frightened note.

"You'll learn all that soon enough," Emily said bracingly. "I believe you're as smart as you're beautiful. And Maria is a good, willing worker. I know you won't have any trouble at all."

At noon, Darcy fed Kenny his lunch while Maria and Emily cooked the midday meal for the adults. Then she took the child to his room and bedded him down for his nap. "Story!" he demanded forcefully.

Darcy chuckled and her sea green eyes sparkled with amusement. "You're as bossy as your uncle, young man." But she gave in to him and, propped up against his pillows, she told him the story of Chicken Little.

Kenny listened in fascination as Darcy mimicked all the farm animals and, when she'd finished, he mumbled sleepily, "Sky fall down."

Darcy smiled and kissed his chubby little cheek. Really, he was a darling, she thought, and in just one short morning he had wormed his way into her heart. She rose from the cushioned chair and put him in his crib. He was already almost asleep.

When she returned to the kitchen, the meal was on the table and Mike was there. Standing beside him was a tall, lean man with a weathered, gaunt face which testified to years of being constantly exposed to the outdoor elements.

"Morning, sweetheart." Mike threw his straw hat on to a spare chair and came over to kiss Darcy lightly. She stiffened at his touch, then remembered it was just an act played for the benefit of the others. "Darcy, I'd like you to meet my foreman, Slim McElroy."

Darcy held out a slender hand and smiled warmly. "I'm pleased to meet you, Mr McElroy."

"Same here, Mrs Trent. But call me Slim. Mister ain't a handle that fits me right, somehow."

Darcy laughed. "Then Slim it is," she agreed.

They all sat down at the table. The men discussed their morning's work. They had taken a few of their hands over to a neighbouring ranch to help with the spring round-up. "Should be finished in a week or so, and then we'll start on ours." Mike grinned at Darcy. "I'm going to be a lousy husband for a few weeks, honey, but we'll make up for it and have our honeymoon later."

Darcy's face flamed, and Slim grinned at her. "It's a mighty understanding woman who'll marry a rancher right at round-up time, Mrs Trent. But I'm sure glad you did. Being married is bound to improve Mike's temper when things go wrong."

Darcy had recovered from her embarrassment. "That bad, huh?" she asked.

"Like an angry Brahman, ma'am. It don't pay to git on the wrong side of Mike."

Darcy smiled demurely. "I believe I'll be able to handle him."

"The devil you will!" Mike protested laughingly.

"But of course, *darling*," she said

tauntingly. "A woman's gentler instincts have tamed man since the beginning of time. Otherwise men would be nothing but uncivilised beasts."

"So I'm an uncivilised beast, eh?" he demanded. His eyes kindled. "We'll see who gets tamed!"

Slim laughed heartily at them both, clearly enjoying himself. Then he politely asked Darcy for seconds on Emily's fried chicken and the talk became general after that. Mike asked Darcy if she had met Kenny yet, and her eyes lit up and sparkled. "He's adorable, Mike. It's going to be fun caring for him."

His eyes studied her for a long moment, but they were half closed, shielding the expression in them. "I'm glad you think so," he said at last. "He takes after his uncle, you know." Seeing her enquiring look, he added, "Being adorable, that is."

When they finished the meal, Slim bade Darcy a polite goodbye and went outside. Mike picked up his hat and then he leaned forward to whisper in Darcy's ear, "So you're going to tame me, huh?"

She couldn't meet his gaze, so her eyelashes fluttered down provocatively. A tiny smile tugged at her lips. "I might," she said softly.

He grinned, then asked, "How'd you sleep last night, Mrs Trent?"

Her eyelids flew up. His meaning was unmistakably clear. He bent towards her again. "I'll be taming you, little wildcat." But before she could think up a retort, he was gone.

Darcy decided to rest for an hour after lunch and then she went with Emily out to a storage room beside the garage.

"This is where I put the things Mr Mike saved from his mother's house when he built the new one. I wanted to throw most of it out, only Mr Mike wouldn't let me. But you can see it's mostly a pile of junk."

"Oh, but Emily, no!" Darcy exclaimed. "Much of this is practically priceless. Look at this old rolltop desk. All it needs is to be refinished."

"Hmmm," said Emily. "I wouldn't have that junk in my house. And all those old vases and churns and irons — what does a man want with all that stuff cluttering up a place for?"

Darcy knew she would hurt the older

woman's feelings if she kept protesting, so she only said, "I imagine he wanted it all because it had been his mother's." And all at once, she had a deep conviction that it was true — that Mike had insisted on keeping all these old things, not so much because of any monetary value to them, but rather because of their sentimental value. It surprised, yet somehow pleased her. She picked up a dust-coated cast iron.

"That belonged to Mr Mike's grandmother," Emily told her. "His mother was just like him about hanging on to old, useless junk."

"A lot of these things must be really old," Darcy said slowly. She had a passion about early American pieces, and though she had never had the money to indulge her interest, she had visited second-hand furniture stores and auctions as often as possible and had studied books from the library on antiques. She sighed as she put the iron back in its place. Her interest in antiques had been another thing which her mother had complained about. "Why do you want to learn about old furniture and dishes and things?" she had demanded querulously. "It's just a stupid waste of time."

Now Darcy looked around her with a deep sense of quiet joy. She spotted a bisque figurine of a young girl; a large old cast-iron pot leaning against the wall in the corner; a Horn of Plenty bowl. She knew that in one way alone could she really repay Mike for all he had done for her and she intended to do it. Little by little, she would take these abandoned treasures of his and find them a rightful setting in his home. It was the least she could do for him.

"What's in this old trunk, Emily?" she asked as she spotted it near the door.

"Old family pictures and books, I think," Emily answered. "Now, I can see some sense in saving them, but the rest of this stuff belongs in the trash pile where it could be burned." She eyed Darcy thoughtfully. "Maybe *you* could talk Mr Mike into it. I'm sure you could use this room in a better way if he'd part with — "

Darcy shook her head. "No, Emily," she said firmly. "If Mr Mike wants to keep all this, we'll honour his wishes."

Emily grumbled as they went back to

the house, but Darcy ignored her. Her mind was busy on the possibilities of redecorating the house, with a view to including as many of Mike's mother's things as possible. The butter churn could hold an arrangement of dried flowers; the bisque figurine would look nice on the mantelpiece in the den. She wondered about the photographs in the trunk. She would go through them soon, she promised herself.

She spent the rest of the quiet afternoon playing with Kenny after he awoke refreshed and lively from his nap. She felt that at the moment, getting acquainted with the baby was more important than attempting to begin taking over her housekeeping duties. After all, Emily and Maria had those jobs well in hand between them and once Emily left, Darcy wanted the child to feel secure in her care.

Mike came home around six, looking hot and tired and dirty. Darcy was in the family room, watching Kenny play with his blocks. When Kenny saw Mike, he abandoned his play and ran to his uncle. "Me build house," he said proudly.

"And it's very nice too," Mike assured

him. Then he picked Kenny up and lifted him above his head. "How are you today, pal?"

Kenny squealed with happiness as Mike threw him in the air, caught him and hugged him before setting him down again. Then his eyes met Darcy's. "I'm tired and want a bath," he said. "Will you fix me a drink?"

Darcy nodded and rose. "What would you like?"

"Scotch and soda." He headed towards the hall. "Just bring it along to my room."

A few minutes later, Darcy knocked timidly at Mike's bedroom door. "Come in," he shouted.

Hesitantly, she opened the door and went inside. No one was in the room. The sound of running water came through the partially opened bathroom door. Darcy stood rooted, not knowing what to do.

Mike came to the door. His face was covered with shaving lather; his chest was bare, revealing thick, dark hair; a long yellow towel draped around his torso. "Thanks a million, Peanut. Just set it on the dresser."

Darcy did as she was told and then

she beat a hasty retreat to her bedroom. She touched her hot face nervously. Mike had looked so vitally masculine, so strong, so — so intimate that way. It had been as though they really were man and wife.

And so they were! With a sense of shock, she sank down on to the edge of the bed. Mike had not seemed the least bit perturbed for her to see him in that half-naked state! They could have been married for years, so casually had he acted. His words from the night before came flooding back. "Marriage is marriage. I have a perfect right to make love to my wife." And the way he had kissed her — had embraced her! She remembered only too well the way she had felt herself responding. And tonight — would he come to her room again? Did he really expect her to give in to him without a quarrel when the entire marriage arrangement was just a business deal? If he did, he would find her just a bit difficult, she decided rebelliously. He would find that the weak, biddable girl from the hospital no longer existed. She would fight him tooth and nail if necessary, but give in to his arrogant assumption that he had a husband's claims — never!

She dressed slowly for dinner in a long blue hostess gown. Then she swept her silvery blonde hair up into a more sophisticated style than she usually wore. There was a light of battle in her eyes and she wanted every shred of self-confidence she could muster, Michael Trent might think he had married a pushover, but she planned to teach him differently!

She returned to the family room to find Mike there, playing with Kenny. He stood up politely when she entered. "Would you care for a drink?"

"Sherry." She sat down on the sofa as Mike moved over to the bar. Emily came in.

"Bedtime, Kenny," she said. "Go and kiss Uncle Mike."

Kenny ran across the room and Mike bent down to receive his kiss and to give him a loving pat on his bottom. He's good with children, Darcy thought in some surprise. He really cares about Kenny. How many other men would have taken on the care of their brother's child like he had? It was a point in Mike's favour, and for some obscure reason it pleased Darcy.

Then it was her turn to be kissed before Emily led Kenny away.

Mike came back and joined her with their drinks. "Well, what do you think of your new home now that you've had time to explore it?"

"Temporary home," Darcy pointed out obstinately.

Mike's jaw tightened. Then, with a slight nod, he silently conceded the point. "Well?"

"It's very lovely," she told him enthusiastically. "And very well laid out. Your architect must have been a very talented one."

"Thank you," he said solemnly.

Darcy stared. "You mean you . . . "

He nodded again and twirled the glass round between his two large brown hands. "I studied architecture in college, but I never got the chance to use it. Dad got sick just before I graduated and he died a short time later. I came home to take care of my mother and the ranch, while Don got his education. He never had the least interest in the ranch, so," he shrugged, "I stayed on and eventually bought out his share."

"And when did you build this house?

Before or after your mother died?"

"After." He grinned wryly. "The old house was in a terrible shape. We'd been after Mom for years to let us build her a new one, but she wouldn't have it. It was the house she'd come to as a young bride and she refused to live anywhere else until she died."

"I — think that's rather wonderful," Darcy said shyly.

Mike looked at her rather oddly. "Do you? Why?"

Darcy spread out her hands in an uncertain gesture. "I suppose because it means she must have been very happy in her home, in her marriage, so that in the end, even though the house was old and unsound, all her treasured memories were stored up there, and she was loath to have them displaced."

"You sound very like her just now," he said thoughtfully. "Not your voice, but your words." He paused for a long moment, then asked in a low voice, "Is that what you want for yourself, Peanut?"

She bit her lip. The conversation had turned so personal. "I — suppose so," she admitted hesitantly. "Yes, I think most women hope to have a life like that — love-filled."

Mike made an inarticulate sound, but when she looked at him he was standing up. "Shall we go in to dinner?"

Darcy nodded and stood too, and the intimate, personal moment was gone.

They spoke of impersonal matters over dinner. They talked about the weather, the ranch, Darcy's redecorating plans, Kenny. But all the while Darcy was nervously aware that it was growing later — that in a matter of a few short hours it would be bedtime. She was very conscious that she did not feel quite so self-confident about fighting Mike now that she sat across from him. He was so absurdly huge and overpowering and she knew that physically she was not one tenth his match in strength. Would he resort to so crude a method as brute strength to get his way? Covertly, when he was not looking, she studied him. Yes, there was an animal strength about Mike — and an animal's streak of cruelty, too.

He looked up and caught her gaze. "What are you thinking about so seriously?" he asked abruptly.

"N-nothing," she stammered. She quickly lowered her gaze to her plate.

But after dinner Mike did not follow her into the living room as she had expected. He stopped her in the hall and said apologetically, "I'm sorry to be deserting you so early, but I've got a lot of accounts to work on tonight." Darcy watched with blank amazement as he crossed over to his study, went in and closed the door.

A firm dismissal it had been. There had been no hint of any desire on his part for a cosy interlude later. Darcy could not decide whether she was angry, amused or relieved. And then she took herself severely to task for allowing herself to fall into such a bewildered state. She should be wildly happy so long as he ignored her. Of course she was. Absolutely. Positively.

6

ON Thursday, Mike drove Darcy into Wilson City for the first time. She went armed with a list of items she needed to begin her redecorating job. Over that, she and Mike had engaged in another brief battle. She wanted to start with his bedroom, but he insisted she had to do her own first. "But I don't see what difference it makes to you where I start," she argued.

"Of course it makes a difference. I'm quite used to living with the mismatched colour schemes Emily threw together, but you're not. I'd like you to be happy with your room, Peanut. Then maybe you won't feel like running away."

"But I wasn't planning on running away," she said crossly.

"Then we'll do your room first just to give you an added incentive to stay."

Wilson City was an old town. The courthouse, which stood in the centre of town, was a three-storied building of faded yellow stone. Dignified old live oaks stood in the courthouse square, casting cool shadows over benches and sidewalks. A number of old men, some in overalls, some in khaki, sat on the benches and smoked contentedly. To a man, they all wore the wide-brimmed Stetson.

The business district was an odd blending of old and new. Impressive old brick or stone fronted several stores, with the name of the store carved in stone above the entrance. Next to them were modern, sleek plate-glass fronted shops. There was a drive-in hamburger stand just across the street from an old red brick school building; a quick stop grocery next to a stately dry goods store. An old railroad track across the main street attested to the years when cattle had been shipped by rail from the district. There was a large modern community swimming pool and a brand spanking new City Hall, landscaped with a profusion of palms and yuccas.

Mike dropped Darcy off in front of a decorator shop. "I've got some ranch supplies to order, so I'll be a couple of hours at least. Meet me at the Wilson Inn at one. We'll have lunch there." He gave Darcy explicit directions on how to reach the restaurant, a wad of money, and an impersonal wave.

Two hours later, as she walked down the street, Darcy felt well satisfied with her morning's work. She had arranged to have a couple of men sent out on Monday to hang the silky green and gold print wallpaper in her room. With them also would come the lime green bedspread and matching draperies, a gold and white bedside lamp and two crystal dresser lamps. The room would be transformed charmingly and she knew the quicker she got hers done, the sooner she could begin on Mike's.

She had been appalled with Mike's room. True, it was spacious, but that was about all that could be said charitably about it. The furniture it held was old and worthless — a relic of his childhood days, she felt sure. The floor was carpeted in deep blue and Emily had seen fit to use a dingy brown bedspread and a sickening shade of yellow for the curtains. It had all been horridly depressing. Darcy fairly itched to throw it all out and start from scratch. Mike deserved a far more pleasant place to rest.

He was waiting for her when she arrived at the restaurant. As soon as they were seated, he looked at her critically and said, "You've actually got some colour in those cheeks at last, Peanut. Was it the hot walk or the excitement of shopping?"

"Both, I suppose," she laughed.

A waitress came to take their order, and when she was gone, Darcy launched into a recital about her purchases. "And Mike, they have the most gorgeous silver I want to have made up into a bedspread for your room. But first, we need to get you some new furniture."

"I agree," he said. "We'll have a go at looking for it next week, okay?"

"Yes. But today before we go home, would you take me to a nursery? I'd like to get some bulbs and flower seeds and maybe a few plants for the patio and . . . "

"Hey!" Mike laughed. "You're going into this decorating thing with a vengeance, aren't you?"

Darcy flushed. "Oh, am I being too extravagant, because if you — "

He held up a hand. "No, no, Peanut, you're nowhere near to breaking me. I'm just surprised, but pleased that you seem to care enough about my home to want to do all this."

"Oh, but it'll be a pleasure," she exclaimed, her eyes glowing. "You've got such a lovely home, if only it's fixed up the way it should be."

He nodded. "Emily's a treasure, but her talents are non-existent in the field of colour co-ordination and decorating, I'm afraid."

"I know," Darcy agreed, "but all the same, I'm going to miss her when she goes. She's a grand person."

After lunch, Mike drove her to the bank. She looked enquiringly at him. "We need to establish you a checking account so you won't need to worry about coming to me when you need money," he explained.

"Oh, but no, Mike! I don't need . . . "

"You do," he said in a final, let's-hear-no-more-nonsense voice. "Come on."

Their business at the bank did not take long and, when they walked out, Darcy carried a cheque book with her name stamped in gold upon it. "Mrs Darcy Trent." It felt strange, but rather pleasant, to know that was how she would be signing her name from now on. It had a nice ring to it.

They left the nursery loaded with plants and patio planters. As they headed towards home, Mike said, "I'll get one of my hands to dig your flower beds tomorrow, Peanut. Just tell him where you want them."

The following morning, Mike held good to his promise. One of the men, who said his name was Buck, arrived at the house immediately after breakfast, and Darcy went outside with him and showed him where she wanted beds dug. Kenny was delighted and rushed inside to fetch his toy bucket and shovel. While he 'helped' Buck dig the flower beds, Darcy settled to work contentedly on the patio, potting her plants. There was an airplane plant, caladium bulbs, which looked rather like dried up onions now, but would eventually turn into beautiful red and white leaves, a tall, lush rubber plant and two or three different types of fern.

By noon the patio had taken on a slightly tropical air. Darcy was determined it should have more plants soon, but she was content with her efforts thus far.

Mike did not show up for lunch and

afterwards Darcy put Kenny to bed for his nap. She returned to the kitchen with a worried expression on her face. "Emily, should I pack a lunch to take to Mr Mike? But I don't have any idea where he is."

Emily shook her head. "No, honey. There's a camp cook for all the hands. When Mr Mike's too busy to come to the house, he just eats with them."

Darcy was relieved. She had been worried about Mike working so hard as he did without any food. Every night she had been here so far, he had come in exhausted.

"Why don't you take a nap, Mrs Trent?" Emily suggested. "We don't want you to get overtired, and you did quite a bit this morning."

"I'm not in the least tired, Emily," Darcy assured her. "I want to poke around in the storage room again. Have you a key to the trunk that's there?"

Emily nodded, opened a drawer and handed her a bunch of keys. "It's that small silver one, I think. But I hope you don't want me out there to go through all that junk! I've got plenty to do in here."

Darcy laughed. "No, I don't need you." In fact, she was happy Emily didn't want to come. It would have been hard to go through all the lovely old things with Emily constantly criticising and suggesting burning the whole.

In the trunk she found a box of family photographs on top, and she sat down and looked through them with curiosity. There were pictures of Mike as a child, along with his brother and two adults who she assumed to be his parents. Mike's hair had always been dark, but the eyes had been more frank then, more open and readable. There was one adorable snap of him holding a large bass on a stringer. He was wearing jeans and a striped pullover and he looked about ten. There were others of him with a dog, on a horse, in his high school graduation cap and gown. She studied the photos of his brother Don and his parents curiously. Don favoured their mother the most; his hair was a light shade of brown, his eyes a blue like his son's. Mrs Trent had a lovely face, a kindly expression, and Darcy suddenly thought wistfully that she would have enjoyed knowing her. Mike's father had been an older edition of Mike himself — tall, though not, Darcy thought as his son, but with the same dark hair, the same inscrutable eyes, the same firm, decisive chin. She wondered idly whether Mike's mother had experienced any trouble understanding her husband, and whether or not he had been gentle with her. And then she realised how silly she was being and laughed at herself.

She had not noticed any family photographs around in the house, so she gathered up a few of the better ones and took them back with her. She would ask Mike if he would like them framed. They would look nice on the shelves in the family room.

Kenny was awake when she got back, demanding, "Outsite." Darcy felt rather hot from the stuffy storage room and wanted fresh air herself, so together they went out to the front lawn.

Darcy sat beneath the huge live oak in the shade while Kenny tossed her a ball and she returned it. There was a strong breeze today and it felt cool on her flushed face; billowy white clouds scuttled in the sky; she could hear the far-away drone of a jet; the leaves of the tree rustled above her head. It was pleasant here, far away from the noises of town life — no constant hum of traffic in front of the house, no loud neighbours screaming or television sets blaring.

A few minutes later, Mike drove up and stopped his pick-up in the drive. "Hi," he greeted them as he unwound his long legs from beneath the steering wheel and stepped out. "Having fun?"

"Me throw ball," Kenny informed him.

"Very well, too," Mike told him. "You'll be the baseball star of the family when you grow up." He walked over to Darcy and dropped down to the ground beside her.

"What are you doing back so early today?" she asked. "When you didn't come for lunch, I decided you must be really busy."

"I was, but we finished early over at Howard's ranch. We'll start the round-up here next week and then I'll be gone so much you'll forget you even have a husband."

Darcy smiled at that and shook her head. "You're far too large and imposing for that."

He grinned at her. "And you, tiny though you are, would be equally difficult to forget."

She could not imagine anything about

herself to be unforgettable and wished she had the courage to ask him what he meant, but now he had obviously forgotten the subject, because he leaned back against the tree trunk, lit a cigarette and asked idly, "How's your day been?"

"Oh, nice. I set out some bulbs and planted the flower seeds and potted the patio plants."

Mike blew a smoke ring into the air. "Since I'm off this afternoon, how would you like to go horseback riding?"

Darcy stared at him. "But — oh, no. I've never been on a horse in my life!"

He laughed. "Well, it's never too late to start. I'll teach you. And I've got a gentle mare you can ride."

"Really?" Darcy's eyes sparkled. "Yes, I think I would like that."

"Then go get into some jeans and sturdy shoes. Next time we get to town remind me to take you to the bootmaker. We need to have some made for you."

She looked down at his own pointed-toe Western boots and, laughing, shook her head. "No, I don't think so. I'd feel ridiculous in them."

"Ridiculous or not, you need them.

They're the most practical thing to wear when you're riding a horse, but another reason is that they're a protection against rattlesnake bites."

"R-rattlesnakes?" Her face paled alarmingly.

Mike laughed. "Don't worry. You're not likely to get bit, but we won't take any chances. We'll get the boots, and any time you happen to go to the pastures or horseback riding, you should wear them."

They both looked up, startled, when a car whipped around the bend in the road and pulled up to a stop in the drive just behind Mike's truck.

Mike got up slowly, and so did Darcy. A tall, elegant girl stepped out of the white automobile. She was wearing white pants and a white blouse, and her hair, almost black, was swept up elegantly from her neck. Long golden rings dangled from her ears. Darcy had never seen a more beautiful creature, and suddenly was self-conscious of her wrinkled skirt and old sweater, of her wind-tossed hair and lack of make-up.

Mike went forward to greet her and she threw her arms around his neck and kissed him soundly. Shock held Darcy rooted where she was.

"Darling," the other girl said now in a low, husky voice, "you haven't called me since your last trip to Austin." A pout puckered her lips, but it was a seductive expression that Darcy wondered how she managed to achieve.

Mike disentangled himself from her embrace, stepped back and dropped a casual arm across Darcy's shoulders as he drew her forward. "Maxine," he said politely, "I'd like you to meet my wife, Darcy. Sweetheart, this is Maxine Roberts, a neighbour of ours."

Maxine did not look at Darcy. She stared blankly at Mike for a stunned moment, and her face drained of colour. "Your wife!" she finally spat out. "I don't believe it!"

"Nevertheless, it's true," Mike said smoothly. Darcy peeped up to see that his firm jaw had hardened into granite. There was something between these two, she realised suddenly. Or there had been. Now he glanced down at her and smiled tenderly. "It was love at first sight with us, wasn't it, Peanut?"

For an instant she was blazingly furious with him, but then she remembered that part of her job was to play act. "That it was, *darling*," she said, just as smoothly as he. Then she turned to smile up at the taller woman. "But we aren't being at all hospitable, Mike," she protested. "Miss Roberts, won't you come in? I'll have Maria bring us some coffee — or tea if you'd prefer?"

"No, thank you," Maxine said ungraciously. "I can't stay." She looked at Mike again and her eyes glittered angrily. "I came to invite you to have a barbecue with us tonight. Dad sent me."

Mike's hand tightened on Darcy's shoulder. "Darcy and I would be delighted to come, wouldn't we, honey?"

Darcy could think of a lot of words she could have used to express her feeling about having dinner with Maxine Roberts, and 'delighted' wasn't one of them. However, obviously Mike wanted to go. And she supposed she had to meet his friends and neighbours sometime. She forced herself to smile. "Yes, of course we would."

Maxine's dark eyes rested on Darcy's face now, for the first time, and there was such open hostility in them that Darcy felt shaken. Then her expression changed swiftly and a smile touched her lips. "Wonderful. About seven-thirty? Then you can tell us all about your sudden marriage."

After she was gone, Darcy felt a hundred questions on her lips, but Mike was wearing his inscrutable expression again and the questions died, unasked. Besides, she knew she had no real right to ask them.

Maxine greeted them that evening wearing a floor-length white culotte pants outfit with a scarlet sash. It emphasised every curve of her tall, elegant frame. Darcy felt dwarfed and totally insignificant in her yellow and white flowered long dress. Tall women had such an advantage over short ones! They looked so graceful and sophisticated. Someone who barely topped five feet one could never aspire to sophistication. And as Darcy watched Maxine greet Mike, she could not help but notice how splendid they looked together — superior, tall, handsome specimens of the human race. Maxine kissed Mike fully on the lips again, as she had that afternoon, and then she smiled down at Darcy. "You mustn't mind my kissing your husband. I claim a lifetime of knowing him as my privilege."

"Oh, I don't mind," Darcy assured her with unruffled calm. "What's a kiss between two very old friends? I should imagine you both shared the same baby carriage."

Since it was obvious that Maxine was several years younger than Mike, the remark was deliberately provocative. Maxine flushed angrily, but recovered herself. "Dad's on the patio with Vince and the Barkers. Shall we join them?" Her back was ramrod straight as she strode on before them.

Mike leaned down and whispered, "Where did you get those claws, Peanut?"

Darcy flushed but refused to answer. Indeed, she couldn't imagine what had come over her. But somehow Maxine's patronage, coupled with her possessiveness over Mike, had brought out an ungovernable instinct to fight back.

For the next hour, Darcy was the centre of attention, which she suspected did not suit Maxine at all. But as each new guest arrived and was introduced to Mike's new bride, she was greeted warmly and with open welcome. Darcy began to understand that Mike was a very popular man with his neighbours.

"How did you happen to meet Mike, dear?" a matronly lady named Mrs Langley asked. "He's kept you such a deep, dark secret from us." All the guests were silent, waiting for her answer. Darcy looked up and met Mike's eyes briefly. She couldn't tell by the look on his face what he wanted her to say. And he'd been so touchy about her gratitude. But stiffly, she resolved not to make up any more fantastic lies than she was obliged to do. The truth would suffice — as far as possible.

"He saved my life," she said gravely. "I was injured in an automobile accident and trapped beneath the car. Mike pulled me away just before it burst into flames."

There were several gasps. Mrs Langley smiled delightedly. "But how utterly romantic! And I suppose," she said archly, turning to Mike, "she was so beautiful and appealing you just naturally fell in love with her."

"Exactly," Mike agreed.

Darcy shot him a suspicious glance but, as he had already turned away to speak to Maxine, he did not notice.

Darcy's attention was claimed next by Vince Kirby, a man who appeared to be in his early thirties, whom she had met when they first arrived. "They're beginning to serve the food. Care to join me?"

"Yes," Darcy smiled at him warmly, "I'd love to." She was filled with relief not to be left alone to make her way to the buffet table. Mike, his head bent in attentiveness to what Maxine was saying to him, had obviously forgotten his duties towards his wife.

Vince laughed as they found a couple of chairs and spare-ribs, pinto beans and potato salad, ignoring her laughing protest that she couldn't possibly eat it all. "You're as thin as a toothpick," he told her. "You need every bite. What's Mike been doing, starving you?"

"On the contrary," she assured him. "And he's been equally as unflattering as you about my looks."

Vince laughed as they found a couple of chairs and sat down near a huge fan-shaped pot plant. "Oh, now, how unfair! You *know* I wasn't criticising your looks. You're absolutely beautiful, you know, and Mike's a lucky dog."

A soft flush spread across Darcy's face. She was not used to men paying her compliments and she was not sure how to respond. He seemed to sense her embarrassment, because he asked in a matter-of-fact voice, "How do you like our part of the state?"

She gave some answer and soon lost her reserve as their conversation hopped from one subject to another. She learned that Vince was a widower and that he, too, was a local rancher, though not, he told her, on such a large scale as Mike. "He has the largest ranch in the county." They discussed movies and books and even entered into a hot discussion about politics, which ended up with them both subsiding with mirth. Darcy had lost all sense of time and place until she was abruptly brought back to the present when Mike's cold voice said, "I think it's time we were leaving, Darcy."

"Oh!" She looked up, startled, and was astounded to see his eyes glittering like cold flints of steel. She rose at once. "Of course. I'm ready to go." She turned to Vince who had risen as well. "It's been a pleasure meeting you, Vince," she said, giving him her hand. "Perhaps we can continue our debate another time?"

Mike was stonily silent in the car as they headed home. The night air was chilly and Darcy hugged her arms around herself. She stole a glance at Mike. His profile could have been carved of marble. What on earth had angered him? "It — it was a nice party, wasn't it?" she finally asked timidly, hoping to break the cold silence that had settled between them.

"Was it?" His voice was cold, hard, uncompromising.

Darcy subsided into silence again. She did not make a second attempt, and the rest of the drive was made in frigid quiet, while she racked her brain to think of something she might have done to offend him. But all at once she felt she knew. Mike had been with Maxine almost all the evening. Were they in love? Had they had a lovers' quarrel and in anger and pique, Mike had married herself instead? And was now regretting it? It all added up — Mike's hard, unapproachable expression, Maxine's shock and later possessiveness. I, Darcy thought depressingly, am in the way — the sharp point in the triangle.

When they entered the house Darcy looked at Mike uncertainly. "I guess I'll go to bed now. Goodnight."

He made no answer and she turned away dispiritedly and went down the hall. But as soon as she stepped inside her bedroom, Mike was suddenly there behind her. He came in and closed the door and then stood there, eyeing her grimly.

"Just what was the general idea," he asked in a deadly quiet voice, "trying to make me look like a fool in front of my friends?"

She gasped and stepped back as though he had slapped her. "How on earth did I do that?" And suddenly she remembered what she'd said to Maxine when they'd first arrived. "Oh," she whispered, conscience stricken. "I'm sorry. But she made me so angry with her patronising tone that I just had to say something back in pure self-defence."

His dark brows snapped down together over his eyes in a quick frown. "What the devil are you talking about?"

Her eyes widened. "Why, Maxine, of course."

His hand sliced across the air in a

negative gesture. "I wasn't referring to that. I'm talking about you spending all the time sitting there alone with Vince Kirby. I told you once," he added in a slow, measured tone, "that I wouldn't stand for any talk about us. And that means you."

"But what did I do?" she demanded, beginning to get angry herself.

"You're a new bride," he said bitterly. "You might remember that generally a new bride doesn't spend an entire evening at a party showering all her attention on a man who doesn't happen to be her husband!"

Hot fury surged through her veins now. "Maybe not," she snapped, "but when that same husband is so engrossed with another woman, and the bride is left rather all on her own in a room full of strangers, she feels mighty grateful for a friendly gesture, no matter who the person is, let me tell you!"

He strode across the space between them and grabbed her wrists in a tight vice. "Don't you get impudent with me!" he gritted through his teeth. "I won't have Kirby hanging around my wife. Is that clear?"

"Perfectly," she retorted. "But if that's the case, you'd better keep Maxine's arms from around *your* neck! If you want this marriage to appear real to your friends, kissing Maxine is definitely *not* the way to go about it!" She squirmed, trying to free herself from his grip.

"Oho," he said, and his face darkened ominously. "Maybe you'd prefer it if I kissed you instead?"

"Don't you dare!"

But he ignored her in his rage. He jerked her into his arms and held her so tight she could scarcely breathe. Slowly, deliberately and with cruelty, his lips came down on hers, hard and demanding, with no tenderness at all. His hands on her back moved down to her hips and pressed her soft body against his hard, taut one. Then one hand slipped around and cupped her breast.

Now she hit at him furiously. "No!" she gasped out. "No! Let me go! I *hate* you!" Her voice was raspy with fury.

Mike let her go abruptly, so that she staggered backward. She put one trembling hand up to her bruised lips. Her face had gone a deathly white as they stood glaring at one another. "I hate you!" she gasped again.

"I don't much care what you think of me," he said, "but you're going to conduct yourself like a loyal wife in the presence of others or, so help me, I'll make you sorry." His eyes raked her up and down insolently, so that hot colour flooded back to her face. "That kiss was just a hint. The next time you step out of line, you'll pay the full price."

7

DARCY stood in the circular drive with Kenny and waved. Emily had dressed in her best Sunday black with a tiny black hat with a feather perched on her white head and now she was sitting beside Slim in the car. He was driving her into Wilson City where she would catch a bus for the first leg of her trip to Oklahoma. A dust cloud rose up on the road as the car made the curve and vanished beyond a clump of feather mesquites. Darcy sighed and turned to go back indoors. She was really going to miss Emily. At least with her constant presence in the house, she and Mike had been able to maintain a polite front, but now that she had gone she knew it would become awkward and difficult between them.

More than a week had passed since the night of the barbecue, and neither of them had done more than speak politely to the other whenever someone else happened to be present. Not that Mike had been around very much anyway. He was busy in the pastures, herding up the cattle, like as not skipping lunch and not arriving at the house until after dark, tired and dirty and hungry, staying awake only long enough to bathe and eat. Darcy clenched her fists as she thought of Mike. How she hated him now! He had stayed constantly at Maxine's side that evening, and then he had had the audacity to accuse her of flirting with Vince — of creating food for gossip. He had a fantastic nerve! And the way he had treated her afterwards in her bedroom — kissing her with such cold cruelty, deliberately humiliating her with his touch! Oh, she could scream with rage whenever she thought of it. She would never forgive him, never!

"Emily gone-gone," Kenny said sadly.

Darcy pulled herself out of her dark mood and stooped down beside him. He was the reason she had not packed up and left Mike immediately after that awful scene between them. Kenny needed her, and she could not bring herself to abandon him. Now she sought to distract him from his loss of Emily. "Let's go inside and help Maria straighten the house," she suggested. "And then maybe we could bake some oatmeal cookies."

"Cookies. Me like cookies."

Darcy hugged him. "Of course you do," she agreed. "All big boys do."

Between them, it did not take Darcy and Maria long to clean the house, and by ten they were done. "What do you want me to do now, Miz Trent?" Maria asked when Darcy and Kenny entered the kitchen.

Darcy looked thoughtful. "Well, you did the washing yesterday. You could — but no, Emily did the ironing and mending." She shrugged and smiled. "Things are really pretty caught up for the moment, Maria. Why don't you just take the rest of the day off?"

Maria's dark eyes lit up eagerly, but then she said, "Oh, but I couldn't! What about lunch and dinner?"

Darcy laughed. "I can cook. In fact, Kenny and I are just about to make a batch of oatmeal cookies. Go on and take some time off. Actually, I enjoy cooking."

"Well — " Maria was doubtful, though it was obvious she was anxious to be gone. "If you're sure? Mr Trent won't mind, will he?"

ASK9   121

"Why should he?" Darcy demanded. "I run the house, not him," she said firmly. "Now take off that apron and go. That's an order!"

Giggling, Maria obeyed. Darcy wrapped the apron around her own waist and pulled a kitchen stool up to the counter. "Let's get to work, Kenny, my boy."

Kenny clambered up the steps and perched on top of the stool. "Me help?"

"Yes indeed, you help," she told him as she lovingly ruffled his hair.

The cookies were a success and Kenny was possessed with impatience as Darcy prepared his lunch and made him eat that before the cookies.

Finally she was able to tuck him in for his nap and then she returned to the kitchen to prepare her lunch and also lunch for Mike, if he bothered to come in. She made a smothered steak with onions, fluffy mashed potatoes, a green salad and broccoli with cheese sauce.

Mike came in at twelve-thirty as she laid the table. His face was red from the heat. "I'll just wash," he told her.

When he returned, the meal was on the table. "Did Emily get off all right?" he asked as they sat down.

"Yes. Slim was at the door at eight. Has he come back yet? I gave him a list of groceries I needed from town."

Mike shook his head while he heaped his plate full. "I gave him a list of supplies I need, too. It'll take him a while." He glanced around. "Where's Maria?"

"I sent her home about ten. The housework is caught up for the moment and I couldn't think of any more jobs for her to do, so I gave her the rest of the day off."

Mike bit into his steak, swallowed and asked, "You didn't keep her to cook lunch?"

"No. I cooked it."

"I thought so. Neither Emily nor Maria has a way with steak this good. It's delicious."

"Thank you," she said politely.

"I had no idea I married a cook."

"There's a lot of things you don't know about me," she answered irritably.

"That's very true," he agreed with chilly politeness.

They finished the meal in silence, and as soon as he was through, Mike picked

123

up his hat and walked to the door. "I'll probably be getting in late tonight, so don't bother waiting supper for me. Just put me a plate of something in the oven."

Darcy didn't answer and he went out of the back door quietly.

The afternoon dragged by slowly. Darcy decided that tomorrow she'd drive into town herself. She couldn't really tackle Mike's room until he helped her pick out the furniture he wanted, but she could start on the family room and the living room. She decided that the kitchen and baths could wait until last.

She compiled a list of things she wanted. More pot plants were needed to brighten up the inside of the house and new sheer green panels to replace the heavy plaid drapes Emily had hung in the family room. Sheer panels would let in more light and not completely obliterate the view of the patio when they were drawn. Picture frames were also needed. Mike had agreed that he would like photographs of his family on the shelves. And lastly canvas and tapestry wool. During the evenings she could work needlepoint chair seat covers for the dining room to replace the dull beige brocade the chairs now wore.

But the list didn't take long and the afternoon stretched endlessly. She and Kenny went for a walk, but it was necessarily a short one, for tiny legs tired quickly.

It was almost nine that night when Mike came in. Kenny had long since been asleep. Darcy quickly prepared supper while Mike bathed and changed — panfried sausage, french fries, fruit salad, beans and a dish of fresh cucumbers. It was not an elaborate meal, but it was difficult to come up with quick meals she could fix whatever time he came in.

His eyebrows lifted in surprise. "You haven't eaten yet?" he asked when he saw she had laid two plates.

Darcy poured tea into two glasses, then added ice cubes. "It's easier, really, to fix it all at once," she said.

Mike sat down. "I told you a plate in the oven would have been okay."

"Not okay with me," she said briskly. "It sounds horrible — all dried out and crisp around the edges. You can't possibly eat that."

"But now you'll be in here so late, clearing everything away," he protested.

"Don't *worry* about it," she all but snapped. "If I don't mind, why should you? Besides," she added without thinking, "I'd rather be doing something than sitting around bored to tears."

His dark eyes half closed as he looked across the table at her. "Is it that bad?"

She flushed, realising what she'd said. "Well," she said candidly, "it was today. But I plan to go shopping tomorrow. I'll get some things to occupy me then."

"Why don't you also go ahead and pick out the furniture you want for my bedroom while you're at it?"

Her eyes widened. "Are you sure?"

He nodded. "I'll be so busy the next few weeks I won't have time."

"Are you sure you trust me?"

Mike grinned crookedly, the first time since the night they had had their fight. It melted some of Darcy's lingering anger. Mike's face was always completely transformed whenever he smiled. "After seeing the job you did on your room, I think I can trust you," he admitted. "Get anything that pleases you. But one thing ... I want a king-size bed." Now his eyes dwelt on her face deliberately, so that the colour rose in her cheeks and it fanned the flames of her anger back to life again.

She lowered her eyes to her plate. "Stop teasing me!" she rasped out.

"Oh, I assure you, Peanut, I'm not teasing. I insist on the king-size bed. Everything else — please yourself."

She glanced up again and saw that he now appeared bored with the topic. Greatly relieved, she stood up and fetched the parfait dessert she'd made.

A couple of days later, when she walked down the gravel drive to the road for the mail, she found, amidst the bunch of envelopes addressed to Mike, a letter for herself. It was from Carolyn Lane, and Darcy tore it open eagerly.

'I guess you're so ecstatically happy that you just haven't cared about writing to friends', she reproached, and a twinge of guilt went through Darcy. She *had* meant to write Carolyn, but at first there just hadn't seemed to be any time, and lately, when there had been time on her hands, and a coldness between herself and Mike, she just hadn't felt like writing. She'd have had to make up a bunch of lies about how great it was to be married, while all the time her heart weighed heavy with the truth that it was all a big mistake.

'*I've been dating Joe,*' the letter went on. '*You know, the best man at your wedding. He's a lawyer here, but not in the least dull and stodgy like lawyers are supposed to be. I think he may be THE ONE!*' Darcy grinned. At least her marriage seemed to have made someone happy. If she had not married Mike, then Carolyn would probably never have met Joe.

'*Write and tell me how ranch life, and marriage in particular, is agreeing with you. But remember . . . if you find you can't handle Mike after all, there's always the sofa in my living room waiting for you. Not that I expect you'll ever need to take up that offer . . . except maybe temporarily, if you ever come up just to visit.*'

Darcy tucked the letter back inside the envelope, entered the house and went into Mike's study to put his mail on the desk. She noticed that the top letter was from Don, his brother. She wondered if Mike wrote to him often, telling him of cute things Kenny had said or done. Once again she thought what a great pity it was that Kenny's mother had died so young. Kenny was a darling, and Darcy loved every minute of caring for him, and she knew Mike did, too. But still, they were not his parents, and the time would come some day when they would have to part. Kenny would go back to his father and probably a procession of babysitter housekeepers, while she herself went . . .

She put a clamp on that thought and went briskly through the house to join Kenny, who played on the patio.

Later that afternoon, when Kenny was fresh from his nap, and Darcy was feeling heartily sick of the house, they walked down behind the barn to the corrals and pens where the men worked.

It was a scorchingly hot afternoon. Darcy's shirt clung damply to her back almost immediately after she left the air-conditioned house. Then, as they neared the corrals, she could see that several pens were jammed with withering bodies of cattle. A great chorus of plaintive mooing filled the air, so that the men were having to shout at one another to be heard; dust rose in great billows, fanning out beyond the pens, carried by a gentle breeze. Darcy could feel the dust settling on her like a brown cape, sticking to her moist skin.

She held Kenny's hand tightly as they approached the fence where they could stand and watch. She could see now that some of the men were herding the cattle through a narrow chute, one by one, and spraying them. A misty vapour hovered over the pen.

Buck happened to walk around them then and he saw her. "Howdy, Miz Trent," he said.

"What are they doing, Buck?" she asked curiously.

"Treating the cattle against parasites ... grubs, lice, ticks. They're spraying them with a chemical solution."

Darcy nodded. "The cattle don't seem to like it very well," she said with a smile.

Buck grinned. "That they don't ma'am. They're an ornery bunch of critters." He touched the brim of his hat politely and went on around the pen.

The vapour lifted momentarily and Darcy saw Mike next to the chute. His blue denim shirt was dark with perspiration. He lifted his hat, rubbed his forehead with the back of his arm, then replaced it.

Darcy could imagine how hot all the men must be. She was wilting herself, and she'd done nothing except walk here. No wonder Mike came in looking so hot and tired and dirty each night. Darcy began to have a reluctant respect for him, and indeed, all these men, who toiled so diligently in the relentless heat. Mike might be a bit of a bully to her, but no one could say he did not dive in and work just as hard as any of his men.

That night, after their supper, Mike called her into his study. When she entered, he was seated at the desk, holding a letter in his hand. "From my brother, Don," he told her, waving the pages slightly.

"I know," she said. "I noticed it when I brought it in." Her brows contracted. "No bad news, I hope?"

He looked up at her and, unexpectedly, smiled. "Oh no, nothing wrong. Merely that he wants some new pictures of Kenny. He keeps me pretty busy taking pictures, I can tell you!"

Darcy grinned. "Well, you can't blame him. Do you want me to take some pictures, then?"

"No, I'll do it. I just wanted to ask if

you'd keep him up a little late from his nap tomorrow. Thought I could do it when I come home for lunch."

"Certainly."

The following day, Darcy made sure that Kenny was freshly bathed and dressed in a clean pair of red shorts and striped red and white shirt when Mike arrived home at noon. The three of them went out to the front lawn. Mike's camera was one of the expensive models with all kinds of knobs and settings. He took a shot of Kenny sitting on a limb of the gnarled old oak; another holding his little bat at the ready; a couple of them with Darcy, though she had protested grumblingly. After all, she hadn't known *her* picture would be taken as well. She had on an old pair of jeans and a plaid shirt, her hair was wind-tossed and tangled and probably all her lipstick was chewed off. But Mike was adamant. Pictures of her he intended to have.

A few moments later Slim happened to pull up in the drive in his pick-up. Mike hailed him before he could drive on back to the garage. "Come and help me, Slim. I've been taking some pictures of my wife and Kenny, but now I'd like a picture of

Darcy and me together. How about it?"

"Well, shore, Mike." He got out of the truck and came across the stretch of lawn towards them. Mike handed him the camera, gave him a couple of directions, and then he ambled over to stand beside Darcy. She threw him a poison dart of a look. "You know I'm not dressed for pictures," she complained beneath her breath. And why, anyway, should he want any pictures of the two of them together? In a normal marriage it made sense, of course, but a temporary one?

"You look fine, Peanut," he said, grinning, "so quit fussing and smile pretty for the camera." Casually, oh, so casually, he draped his arm around her shoulder and pulled her up against his chest. "Okay Slim. Shoot!"

On Sunday, when Mike came in at noon, it was with the announcement that he was taking the afternoon off. "And you and I, my sweet, are going for that horseback ride we never got around to taking."

"Are we?" Darcy demanded, with a lift of her eyebrows at his overbearing way of telling her.

"We are," he said quite definitely. "So

go and change, and be quick."

Darcy obeyed. True, he was overbearing and bossy, but she'd overlook it this one time. After all, she'd been longing to go, so why cut her nose off to spite her face?

Mike mounted her on a brown mare he called Lilli Bell. Darcy leaned forward and stroked her neck. Already, it felt exhilarating to be astride a horse's back! Her eyes sparkled and Mike looked at her with amusement and grinned. "I believe you're excited, Peanut."

She stuck out her tongue at him. "Well, I am, and I'm *determined* not to let you spoil it for me."

He laughed, then swung one long leg easily across the saddle of his own horse. His horse was a beautiful black stallion, and Darcy gazed at it admiringly. "What's his name?" she asked.

His eyes darkened with suppressed laughter. "Trigger," he told her solemnly.

"Trigger?" Her face was blank a moment, then she burst out laughing. "Like Roy Rogers' Trigger?"

"The same. Of course my Trigger doesn't look like his, but . . . " he shrugged. "Dad gave me my first horse when I was ten.

At that time I fairly worshipped Roy Rogers, so naturally I named my horse after his."

"Naturally," she agreed, chuckling.

"So after that, I simply named every horse I ever had for myself, Trigger. I guess you might call it almost superstition. They've all been wonderful horses for me, so I kind of hate to tempt fate by changing it now."

Darcy giggled. "Who'd ever have believed *you* could be so superstitious? It's a wonder you don't wear six-shooters as well."

He laughed. "Probably would if the law allowed."

They set out at a slow walk, Mike giving her instructions about how to handle a horse. "You have to let them know who's boss from the start, Peanut. Don't ever be afraid of them. If you are, they'll sense it at once."

They ambled along pleasantly for a while, not talking as they moved through mesquite and cactus, across rocks and dead tree limbs strewn among the grazing grasses.

"I watched the cattle spraying the other day," Darcy told him suddenly. "There's an awful lot that goes into ranching, isn't there?"

He nodded. "Yes. Some folks think all there is to it is sticking a few head of cattle into a pasture and leaving them to eat the grasses. I wish it was that easy. We also have to inoculate the animals against disease, dehorn them, brand them, have them tested for brucellosis. You worry about droughts and freezes. Today we were separating the young ones from their mothers . . . those that are weaned. Oh, I meant to tell you, we have two new baby calves. If you like, I'll take you and Kenny to see them when we get back."

Darcy's eyes glowed. "Oh, I'd love it. And I know Kenny will be thrilled."

The ride took them across the pasture, through a grove of small live oaks and down to a meandering creek. Mike slid off his horse gracefully, then helped Darcy down. As he held her in his arms for that brief moment, their eyes met, their gazes held. Darcy held her breath, waiting, but when he set her down and her feet touched solid ground, an inexplicable feeling of loss assailed her. His strong arms were no longer around her, his eyes no longer gazed into hers with some wordless message, his lips, those sensuous lips that could be tender or cruel, were no longer tantalisingly close to hers. He had not attempted to kiss her, and she wondered suddenly why it left her feeling incomplete and more than a little disappointed.

Mentally, she shook herself. It was a crazy way to feel. It had been sheer physical infatuation — that was all it was. Had she not hated him that night in her room when he *had* kissed her? But she did not, she acknowledged to herself, feel hate now — not any more.

She walked down to the edge of the creek, dabbled her hands in the water and cooled her hot cheeks. When she stood up and turned around, Mike was leaning against a tree trunk, lighting a cigarette. She went back and sat down beside him. A butterfly darted away among the weeds nearby and she watched it idly.

"What are you thinking about, Peanut?" he demanded suddenly.

Darcy shifted her gaze back to the stream. "I was thinking," she said honestly, "that I envy you."

"Envy me?"

She nodded and swept her hand in an arc. "All this — a wonderful ranch, outdoor living, a place like this to come to when you want to be alone. None of the cramped feeling you get from living in a city, or even a small town like I lived in."

His eyes flickered and then the eyelids lowered, shielding his eyes, so that she could not tell what he was thinking. "Tell me more about your life," he commanded softly: "Did you have swarms of boy-friends?"

She grinned at that, but shook her head. "No. There was no time, and besides — Mom didn't want boys around. So it was kind of difficult." Her voice trailed off, then she turned to look at him fully. "There's nothing much to tell about me," she said flatly. "Tell me about you and Don when you were boys. And tell me this — Did your mother ever manage to cut you down to size?"

He chuckled and unexpectedly he lifted a hand and traced a finger down her cheek. "She managed that fine, just as you seem well able to do."

"Me?" She laughed and shook her head.

"I may try but . . . "

"You manage," he stated emphatically. "I may attempt to come the bully over you, but you . . . "

"You do!" she breathed. "Oh, you can be such a beast sometimes."

He laughed again. "I told you I'd tame you, little wildcat. And I fully intend to."

Her eyes blazed. "Not if I tame you first," she retorted.

"Never," he told her. "You may manage me well enough in some ways, but tame me, never!" And she had to acknowledge to herself that that was probably true.

The next hour passed pleasantly as they lounged there, beside the creek, its music against the rocks a background to their soft voices.

Darcy was happy as they rode back home. Mike had put himself out to be charming this afternoon and she had enjoyed every minute of his company. Mike himself looked contented and relaxed.

When they entered the house, Maria met them with the news that Vince Kirby was in the family room waiting for them.

Darcy preceded Mike into the room. Vince rose from his chair and smiled warmly at her. "Hello, Darcy. I came by to bring you some of my books. Several of the latest best-sellers I thought you might enjoy reading."

"And what," Mike's cold, hard voice said from behind her, "makes you think my wife needs your books? I'm perfectly capable of buying her all the books she wants."

8

THREE days later the furnishings came for Mike's bedroom. Darcy showed the men where to place the furniture, and another man came from the decorator's shop to hang the new drapes with threads of blue shimmering in the silver depths. After the men left, she made up the new king-size bed, topping the sheets and blanket with the beautiful silver spread she had chosen. She set out the new lamps and brought in the blue and white pitcher of Mike's mother's she had found in the store room. It was now a container for a vivid green ivy. She set it on the dresser, then backed off to view the room as a whole. It was lovely, just as she had known it would be, with milk white and sunshine yellow accessories, but she took no pleasure at all in it. In fact, she had taken pleasure in nothing these past few days — not since that wonderful afternoon she had spent with Mike and they had returned to find Vince waiting for her.

Mike had been coldly furious and had almost immediately muttered some excuse and left the room. Shaken by his anger and rudeness, Darcy had been hard put to it to sit there and be a polite hostess. But Vince had seemed oblivious of Mike's snub and he had stayed for an hour and a half, drinking coffee and chatting. "You must get Mike to bring you over some time and see my place, Darcy," he told her eagerly. "I'd like to know what you think of it." He paused and shook his head. "My wife died four years ago and since then the house is nothing but a huge, empty shell."

"Perhaps you'll marry again one day," Darcy said gently.

"I would if I could have the right girl. Only now I've found her, she's already married."

Darcy looked up, startled. His meaning was unmistakable. Her eyes were troubled while she struggled, trying to think of some answer to make. Vince leaned forward and asked earnestly, "What's behind this marriage of yours to Mike, anyway? It was all so sudden and so secretive. And everybody around here believed he would marry Maxine when he ever did get around to marrying anybody."

"Why, there's no secret," she answered shakily. "You heard how we met. I was in a car accident and Mike saved my life."

"But why marry you?" he asked harshly. "Surely it hardly called for that?"

Darcy coloured angrily. "You're not being very flattering to me, are you?" she asked coldly. "But I assure you Mike wasn't forced into marrying me. He married me of his own free will."

Vince looked at her, saw her indignant anger and suddenly he smiled. "I didn't put it very well did I? I made you angry. I'm sorry. Of course Mike would want to marry you — any man would." He laughed now. "I only wish I'd been the guy to save you from that car!"

Darcy laughed, lightening the tension, and offered Vince another cup of coffee.

That night Mike had pitched into her again in the same way he had done the night of the dinner party at Maxine's, and nothing she said could convince him that she had not known Vince was coming and that indeed she had not planned it. Since then they had been frigidly cold to each other, speaking with exaggerated

143

politeness whenever they were obliged to speak at all.

Why was the man so stupidly hung up on Vince Kirby? Darcy thought. Vince meant nothing to her, outside of a pleasant acquaintance, yet Mike blew their innocent relationship all out of proportion. She might almost believe Mike was jealous if she did not know with cold certainty how ridiculous that was. With Maxine around, there could be no competition for his affections at all. So why was he so ready to believe the worst of her? As if she would really encourage another man while she was married, even if that marriage was merely temporary. As if she wanted to create gossip for his friends! If he had such a low opinion of her character as that, then why had he picked on her to marry in the first place?

Darcy's pride, and something more she could not define, was hurt, and she knew that this time she would not thaw quite so readily whenever he might choose to be friendly again. Once bitten, twice shy. She would be careful in the extreme from now on to show Vince, and indeed, any other man, only the scantest of polite attention, but at the same time she determined never to let her guard down with Mike again. She would not let him have the power to hurt her like this.

So now, whenever she had to be near him, she was stiff with reserve and wary caution. For Mike's part, he was cold, indifferent and, when he could, maintained a stony silence. It was a rotten state of affairs, and if it had not been for Kenny, and also her promise to stay for the proposed time, she would have flung in the towel. But a remnant of deeply ingrained commitment made her resolve to stick it out. She had promised – and a promise, in her book, was a promise.

One evening late, as she sat in the family room watching television and working on her dining room seat covers, Mike came in from his study. She looked up in surprise. Lately, as soon as dinner was over, he would shut himself up inside the study until bedtime, so as to avoid her. Tonight was a variation from the usual. He carried a thick envelope in his hand and he came over and dropped it into her lap. "The pictures we took. I thought you'd like to see them before I send them on to Don."

"Oh. Oh, yes, of course." She opened the envelope, pulled out the photos and silently shuffled through them. They had all come out well, including the ones Slim had taken of her and Mike together. A pang went through her as she looked at one of them — Mike, with his arm across her shoulder, smiling, and she was laughing. They looked so happy there. It was a dramatic contrast with the cold reality of the present.

"They're all very good," she said now as she put them carefully back inside the envelope. "Are you sending them all to Don?"

"All of the ones of Kenny. I thought I'd send him one of the two of us."

Darcy looked up at him curiously. "Have you told your brother that you're married?"

His jaw seemed to tighten; his eyes were black coals. There were new lines, she noticed, across his forehead. "Of course I have," he answered. "I wrote him right away and told him."

She looked down at her hands, then boldly met his his gaze again. "And did you tell him your reasons for getting married?"

146

His eyes narrowed. "What reasons?" he asked coolly as he took back the envelope from her.

"That you married me to care for his son. Surely he should know what a great sacrifice you made for him."

He stood a little away from her and now he put both hands on his hips. "I didn't consider it necessary to tell Don the circumstances of my marriage. I prefer him, as well as anyone else, to look on my marriage as normal. But as for this self-sacrifice you mention, I don't go in for the martyred bit. I had my own reasons for marrying you, but sacrifice wasn't any part of it, I assure you." He nodded curtly and went out of the room.

She supposed Mike had spoken nothing more or less than the truth. What he had meant was that she had no vital part in his life at all, that she had not changed his life in any way, so he could not consider their arrangement to be any sort of a sacrifice on his part because he had not given up anything by marrying her. The marriage was to be temporary only, and once it was done with, he would in all likelihood marry Maxine, whom he should have married in the first place. She wondered suddenly if he wanted her out of the way. But if he did, he had only to say the word and she would leave immediately. And she knew that he and Maxine kept in touch. Only last night she had heard him speaking to her on the telephone.

Dispiritedly, she got up slowly and took herself off to bed.

The following evening Maxine telephoned again. Mike took the call in his study, but almost immediately came into the kitchen, where Darcy was still clearing away the dishes, and said, "Maxine's on the phone. She wants to know if you'd like to go into Wilson City with her tomorrow shopping."

Darcy stared at him, but then she shook her head. "Oh, no, I don't think . . . "

"I think you should go — do you good. You've been stuck here in the house a lot lately. Maria can look after Kenny all right."

Stubbornly, she shook her head again. The last thing she wanted to do was spend a day with Maxine. But Mike was getting angry. She could tell by the look on his face. "For heaven's sake, girl, she's trying

148

to be friendly. You can't turn her down."

"You really want me to go?" she asked now, quietly.

He nodded.

"All right," she said at last, reluctantly.

"Good. Go and tell her so. She's waiting on the line."

Darcy prayed for a late blizzard, a rainstorm, anything to cancel the proposed shopping trip, but the next morning when she awoke, the sun was shining brightly and several sparrows chirped gleefully outside her window. "Oh, shut up!" she muttered grouchily to them.

Two hours later she was dressed and ready when Maxine drove up in the white car. Again, Maxine was wearing white, this time a dress, with a green pendant necklace, and a bracelet and earrings to match. Her shoes and bag were also green. Darcy decided white must be Maxine's affectation, with colours being used only as accessories. And as usual, Maxine looked gorgeous, so that Darcy felt plain as one of those pesky sparrows next to a swan in her neat beige dress with the pleated skirt she had thought so smart when she had bought it in Austin. Now she wished

149

she had never laid eyes on it.

"Morning," Maxine greeted brightly. "I'm in one of those buy-the-town-out moods. How about you?"

Darcy managed a smile. "Well, I wasn't planning to get quite that carried away."

Maxine lifted a quizzical eyebrow. "What? Is Mike being the stingy husband?"

Darcy smiled. "On the contrary, I've been spending quite a lot of his money lately. Little by little I'm redecorating the house. We can't live with Emily's colour schemes, you see."

"That's funny. Mike managed to live with them quite well until his marriage." Maxine made it an accusation, as though Darcy was wantonly destroying all he held dear.

"That's because he had no one he could trust to do the job for him before," Darcy answered coolly.

Maxine's face flushed slightly, and Darcy suddenly felt sorry for her. With swift insight, she realised that Maxine must have fairly itched all this time to take over that job for Mike, but she never had been asked. Had it been because Mike wanted to spare Emily's feelings? Or was it because he had simply never wanted Maxine to decorate his home? She sighed quietly. She was never likely to know.

After that one dig at her, Maxine put herself out to be friendly. She gossiped about several of her friends whom Darcy had met that night of the barbecue, told her a little about local politics and described several civic projects in which she was involved. Almost in no time the big white automobile was entering Wilson City.

Maxine whipped up and down several tree-shaded streets with the careless assurance of a native and at last drew to a stop in front of a dress shop. "There are only three shops in town that carry any decent clothes," she said. "Come on, we'll visit them all today and then you'll know where to go whenever you're in town alone."

Darcy trailed inside behind her. She could tell at a glance that it was an exclusive place. A haughty-looking saleslady approached and her face suddenly transformed. "Ah, Miss Roberts," she said gushingly. "How nice to see you again. May I help you?"

"I want to look at some slacks and

blouses," said Maxine. "But first I'd like to introduce you to Mrs Trent. Darcy, this is Edna."

Edna acknowledged Darcy politely and then she helped Maxine select several outfits to try on. Darcy wandered over to a rack of evening dresses. There were every kind — the young, ingénue evening dresses, daring cocktail dresses, dinner dresses. Darcy looked through the latter, thinking that it might be a good idea to buy a really nice one. She already possessed several long dresses, but none were really elegant.

Edna joined her as Maxine went off to the fitting room. "Have you found something you like, Mrs Trent?"

"I'd like to try on this dress," she said now, holding up a black one. "And maybe this pink one as well."

Edna escorted her to a dressing room, vanishing as Darcy struggled out of the beige, but returned almost immediately with two more gowns. "You must try this silver one, Mrs Trent. With your hair, your complexion — " She left the sentence hanging in mid-air, but with an unmistakable meaning.

In the end, Darcy bought the silver. The black had been a little too harsh against her pale white skin, the pink had made her look sallow and sickly, the white was a bit too colourless, but the silver was all one could ask for. It was deceptively plain with a scooped neck, sleeveless and with an empire waist that emphasised her breasts. The long skirt flowed smoothly over her slim hips and legs. The colour brought out shining highlights in her hair, and it subtly flattered her soft, translucent skin. "I'll take it!" she said impulsively.

The rest of the morning was spent pleasantly, going from one shop to another. Maxine bought clothes at each stop, though Darcy, suddenly conscience-stricken over the amount she had parted with over the silver dress, put a firm clamp on her impulses and refused to buy another thing for herself.

They had lunch at a hotel restaurant and while Maxine went off to keep a hairdresser's appointment, Darcy shopped at a department store for some new summer shorts and shirts for Kenny.

On the drive home, Maxine asked what

she had bought during the afternoon. "Oh, just a few clothes for Kenny," she said. "He's growing so fast."

Maxine said in a bored tone, "How very maternal."

Darcy felt herself bristling. "Well, after all, he *is* my responsibility."

Maxine shot her a shrewd look. "I believe that's the only reason Mike married you." She was silent for a moment, then went on, "Yes, I see it all now. He needed a babysitter and housekeeper with Emily leaving, and what better way than to marry someone like yourself who's willing to do the job?"

"Naturally caring for Kenny is my job," said Darcy. "He's Mike's nephew and I'm Mike's wife."

"Wife!" Maxine all but spat the word out. "Mike only married you because you're useful to him at the moment. But it won't last. He's in love with me, he has been for years."

"Then why didn't he marry you?" Darcy asked stiffly. Her hands trembled and she held them tightly in her lap.

Maxine smiled thinly. "We quarrelled. And of course Mike knew I wouldn't be willing to take on the job of babysitting for another man's child. He wouldn't dream of imposing on me so. But once the child is gone, it'll be me he'll want again! You'll have nothing to offer him then. Mike wants a woman who's his equal — who understands his problems with the ranch — someone who can share and understand his life fully."

Darcy realised that that was probably the truth and though she had told herself that many times before, it plunged her into a profound depression to hear it from Maxine herself. *If Mike loves Maxine he'll go back to her after I'm gone*, she thought drearily. It was at that moment she realised that the cruellest trick of all had been played on her by Fate. She loved Mike herself!

"Well, can you deny what I've just said?" Maxine cut in triumphantly on her thoughts.

Darcy pulled together the tattered shreds of her pride. "I see no reason to deny or confirm anything you happen to believe. But the fact remains," she said gently, because now in her newfound knowledge she could still find it in her to sympathise with Maxine's own personal heartache, "I am his wife."

Those words came back to haunt her again that evening as she prepared their late supper. "I am his wife." Every fibre of her being quivered with an agonising desire for it to be so in every sense of the word. But the melancholy truth was that it was still a business arrangement only. Nothing had altered that fact. Indeed, only she herself had altered at all. Mike still believed she was interested in Vince Kirby — and the only reason he resented it was because it might make him look a fool before his friends. All he was interested in was preserving his pride. He had no feeling at all for herself.

She attempted to keep her gaze averted when they sat down to their late meal together. Her discovery was too new, too painful. She had not had time to build a defensive shield, and she was terrified that he might guess the truth — and at all costs she had to keep that from happening.

9

SEVERAL weeks went by and Mike was extremely busy on the ranch. Darcy saw little of him. She was busy, too. Some of the beans and peas from the garden had matured and she and Maria worked hard to get them all into the freezer. Soon the tomatoes would be ripe, and that would be another big job. Darcy was also busy sewing new panels for the patio door, working on her needlepoint chair covers, and shopping often for groceries or supplies for Mike, besides looking after the house and Kenny.

Darcy felt a need to stay occupied every single moment. Whenever she was idle, heartbreak and disillusion set in. It was an intolerable situation, loving Mike so, knowing she was legally his wife, yet knowing, too, that he would never be likely to feel anything for her except indifference. She might as well be a useful piece of the furniture these days for all the notice he took of her.

Yet was not that better than if he paid attention to her, or worse yet, was *kind*? Because that would be her undoing for certain. No, it was far better for them to maintain aloofness.

She lost weight, and there were dark smudges beneath her eyes from sleepless nights, but still each day she drove herself to the utmost. If her smile was brittle and her eyes glazed, there was no one to notice except Maria, who kept silent.

But then several neighbouring ranchers' wives began to visit her, and Darcy was grateful for their readiness to accept her into their midst. Talking with others kept her thoughts away from herself. Mrs Langley, whom she had met at the barbecue, was especially nice. She carried Darcy and Kenny off to church one Sunday morning in Venture and introduced her to others. Soon she was involved in the church bazaar, and this pleased her, too. Any work was welcome.

One evening early in June, Mike came in around six. It was the first time in weeks that he had been home before dark. Just as he had done once before, he said to Darcy, "I'm tired and need a bath. Will you bring a drink to my room?"

She nodded and went to mix the drink. She was nervous as she tapped at his door, but this time he did not appear at the bathroom door. Instead, he called out, "Just put it anywhere, thanks."

She set it on the dresser and hurried down the hall to the kitchen.

When they sat down at the table together for their evening meal, Mike looked at her keenly. It was the first time he had really looked at her for weeks. Now he frowned, his dark eyebrows clamping down ominously over his unfathomable eyes. "You're thinner again, and you look tired. Are you getting sick?"

Darcy denied it. "Oh, no, I'm perfectly fine."

"Then you must be working too hard. What the hell do you have Maria here for? Let her do more of the work."

"She does her share," Darcy said defensively.

"You look tired to death."

Her eyes flashed angrily now. "I'm fine, honestly. So drop it, will you?"

He continued to look at her thoughtfully. "Things are slowing down for me now.

I had thought perhaps it was time we threw a dinner party for some of our neighbours, but I don't know. You don't look up to it."

"Of course I'm up to it," she said indignantly. "When do you want to have it and whom do you want to invite?"

"Any time you say," he answered, "and I thought we'd invite Maxine and her father, the Langleys, the Carters and — " he paused significantly "Vince. I guess I was pretty rude to him that day. And he *is* a good friend of mine, as well as yours."

Her face grew hot. "You don't need to invite him on my account," she said.

"I know," he said quietly. "I just said he's a friend of mine. Well, what do you think of the idea? Shall we give a party?"

"Of course," she agreed very blandly. But her mind was in a seething turmoil. Her immediate reaction was that Mike was planning the entire thing just so he could be with Maxine again. But even though she guessed that he was asking her to give a dinner party as an excuse to see the woman he loved, she knew, for her own pride's sake, she would do the best she possibly could. Because when she did leave, she did not want Mike or anyone else to be able to say she had shirked on her job in any way. Oh, pride! What cold comfort it offered. Yet it was all in the world she could claim for herself.

They decided on the next Saturday night for the dinner, and Darcy worked frantically all week cleaning the already spotless house, polishing, waxing. Everything had to be exactly perfect. She was Mike's wife, and the guests would judge her by that fact. She planned the menu with Maria carefully and on Friday she drove into Wilson City for the groceries and to have her hair done. She would have done it on Saturday, but a ninety-mile drive for a hair-do was just too much extra on the day of the party itself.

And then on Saturday morning the blow fell. Maria showed up at the kitchen door as Darcy was preparing Mike's breakfast. Her eyes were watery and weak-looking; she had a sweater on, despite the mild, silky warm early morning air.

"You're ill!" Darcy exclaimed, once she had looked at the girl.

Maria nodded miserably. "Yes, ma'am. Felix says it must be the 'flu. But I came anyway because you have so much to do today."

"Well you can just turn around and go straight back home to bed," Darcy ordered. "You're in no condition to help me — besides, Kenny might catch your germs. Don't worry about me, I'll manage fine without you."

Mumbling apologies for getting sick at such an inopportune time, Maria soon left. Darcy turned back to the skillet and the bacon that was sizzling. Something akin to panic seized her. How on earth would she manage the dinner party with no help? Oh, this was dreadful! But then she told herself sternly to calm down. She could manage the cooking easily. The house was clean and she had merely to make the beds and straighten things a bit. The only problem, then, was serving the dinner. Maria was to have done that. Now, it appeared, she would have to do it herself.

Mike came in, clad in his work clothes, levis, faded blue shirt, boots. He threw his straw hat on to a spare chair and sat down at the table.

Darcy carried him a cup of hot, strong coffee. "Maria has 'flu," she announced.

"She won't be here today."

Mike looked at her with real consternation. "And the dinner tonight! You'd better cancel it — it'll be too much for you."

"Nothing of the sort!" she exclaimed as she set his plate of bacon and eggs in front of him. "I can manage just fine."

"Are you sure?" he asked with evident concern. "I don't want you to get too tired. You might come down sick yourself."

There it was, she noticed — the *kindness* in his voice again. It was the first time in weeks that he had shown it. He had not sounded this way the other night when he was harping on her health. Unexpectedly, tears stung the back of her eyelids. She turned quickly back to the stove, poured herself a cup of coffee, then stood there for a moment to get control of herself.

When she joined him at the table, she was smiling. "I won't get too tired or sick, either," she assured him. "I feel great, and I *want* to go ahead with the dinner."

"Well, if you're sure," he said dubiously.

That morning she worked like a whirlwind. First Darcy had to prepare the Swiss cream tortes for dessert. Then

163

she straightened the house. That was a little difficult because Kenny, today of all days, seemed a little out of sorts. He followed Darcy around like a little lost soul, whining and fretful.

Mike ate with the ranch hands to save Darcy having to cook at noon, so after she had fed Kenny his simple meal, tucked him in for a nap, and eaten a quick sandwich herself, she went to the telephone and called Mrs Langley.

She poured out her problem quickly and ended with, "I wondered if you knew of someone who would serve the dinner for me."

"I'm sure I can find someone, dear, but it might be several hours before she could get there. And you're having to do it all yourself. Are you sure you don't want to postpone the dinner?"

"No," Darcy said firmly. "I can manage fine if I can get someone to help with last-minute preparations and serve."

"I'll see what I can do," the older woman said.

Darcy returned to the kitchen and set out the ingredients for coq au vin — cognac, Burgundy, fresh mushrooms. There would also be buttered parsleyed potatoes, asparagus amandine and a salad.

At four Mrs Langley called back. "Our foreman's daughter, Rosa will help you. But Darcy, she's only seventeen. You'll have to explain to her carefully exactly what to do."

"That's fine," Darcy breathed. "Thank you so very much!"

Half an hour later Rosa was there. Together they went over the menu, Darcy explaining what Rosa would have to do to the food just at the last moment and how to serve it. Rosa was a willing girl and followed all Darcy's instructions carefully. Darcy felt hopeful. She thought that everything would work out all right.

At six, when Mike came in, Darcy was feeding Kenny and Rosa was washing up a few dishes. "Everything under control?" he asked, eyeing Rosa's back quizzically.

"Fine," Darcy answered. "Mrs Langley helped me get Rosa for tonight." She didn't add that Rosa had to leave by nine-thirty so she could be home to help her father get the other children to bed. Her own mother was in the hospital in Wilson City, having just given birth to a new baby.

165

Darcy finally got Kenny to bed and then she had to rush over her own bath before the guests arrived.

But she took her time over her make-up and hair, and then at last she slipped on the silver dinner dress she had bought. It completely transformed her from the drab girl she had been all day in the kitchen into someone quite different, someone almost, she dared to think, elegant. She began to get excited now. Her cheeks glowed with a heightened colour and her sea green eyes sparkled. She sprayed on cologne, then stood back. She needed one more thing, she decided, as she studied herself critically in the mirror — a touch of jewellery was required. She chose the pearls Mike had given her as a wedding gift. Until now they had lain in their box, unworn. Now they glowed with a life of their own around her neck, and Darcy felt suddenly elated. She looked good and she felt good. Her confidence, which had deserted her for a long while, now came flowing back.

Mike was waiting for her in the family room. He looked so tall and handsome in his dinner jacket, she thought. He stood with a glass in one hand, a cigarette in another, looking out of the patio window. When she entered, he turned, looked at her for a long, silent moment, and then seemed to suck in his breath. He set his glass down on a nearby table, dropped the cigarette into an ashtray, strode forward and took both her hands into his. "You're beautiful tonight, Peanut. Really beautiful." His dark eyes bored into hers intently.

She laughed shakily. "Then my new dress is a success?"

He laughed huskily. "I'll say it is! And I'm glad you're wearing my pearls."

They continued to gaze at one another. Darcy felt bemused, almost as though this was all a dream dredged up out of the depths of her longing. Mike's hands pulled her closer and then he bent his head slowly.

The doorbell rang suddenly, abruptly. Mike's head went up, he dropped her hands, and with a muttered, "Damn!" he went to answer the door.

Darcy bit her lip in consternation. She felt so frustrated that tears were not far away. Mike had been about to kiss her, but the magical moment was lost now.

Somehow she got a grip on her emotions

and then she moved through to the living room where Mike was greeting the Carters.

The dinner went well. The food was good and Rosa served efficiently. Darcy accepted gracefully the compliments paid on her hostess efforts, but all the joy in the evening had gone out for her the moment Maxine arrived. Although Maxine did not monopolise Mike completely all evening, she did the next thing to it. She was constantly at his side, and whenever her glance happened to reach Darcy, there was a mocking look on her face. Darcy felt it was almost as though Maxine were saying "He's mine, you see. He may be married to you at the moment, but he's mine. He always has been; he always will be."

But Darcy's pride came to the fore, and no one could have guessed how depressed she actually was as she moved around in the living room after dinner having a word with each of her guests, seeing that they had coffee, that each was comfortable, that conversation flowed smoothly. But in the back of her mind she only longed for the evening to end.

Vince, who had been sitting and chatting with Mr Roberts, joined her by the window when Mike sat down to talk with the older man. "You're very lovely tonight, Darcy," he told her quietly.

"Thank you." Her reply was automatic.

"How have you been getting on?"

"Oh, very well. In fact, I've been quite busy lately . . . "

"I'd like to talk to you alone," he said abruptly, with his eyes strangely intent on hers. "Could you show me your patio?"

"Oh no!" Panic struck her at the thought. Mike would go through the roof! "I'm afraid I can't leave my other guests, Vince," she said reproachfully. "You must realise that."

"Then when — and where?" His voice lowered intimately. "I know you aren't happy here." He nodded ever so slightly towards Maxine and Mike, who were sitting on the sofa beside Mr Roberts. "She intends to get him back, you know," he said bluntly. "And I love you, Darcy. I must see you alone!" His voice was urgent, husky.

"No!" Her voice was as low as his, so that no one could possibly overhear them, but an edge of impatience tinged it. "I'm Mike's wife," she added now. "You have no right to speak to me like this. No matter what you or Maxine think, I'm still his wife and I won't see you alone. I'm sorry." She moved away from him, conscious that Mike's eyes had been on them. She was also conscious that Mike's appraisal of Vince's motives towards her had been right, for all she had merely thought him casually friendly. Now she had a double reason for staying clear of Vince. She was sorry if he thought himself in love with her, if he might get hurt, but she had no feeling at all for him and she would have to make that plain to him.

It was a little after eleven when the last guest left. Mike and Darcy stood in the doorway, waving them off, and Mike's arm was draped casually about her. With exquisite pain she relished the touch of his hand on her bare shoulder. His thumb was rubbing back and forth absently, sending little thrills shooting through her.

Yet the moment the door was closed, she moved away from him abruptly. "It was a good party, don't you think?" he asked as he busied himself locking the door.

"Yes. Yes, it was."

"How about a nightcap?" he asked now, turning towards her.

She shook her head. "No, thanks. I'm going to change so that I can do the dishes."

"The dishes? But didn't the girl you hired do them? What was she here for?"

"To serve." She shrugged her shoulders. "She could only come if she left at nine-thirty to help her father get the younger children to bed. It's all right," she added as she noticed his quick frown, "I don't mind."

She changed into a cotton overall and house slippers and went to the kitchen. She was filling the sink with hot, sudsy water when Mike appeared. His coat and tie were gone; his shirt sleeves were rolled up above his elbows. He grinned. "Where's a spare apron? I'll help you."

"It's not necessary," Darcy said stiffly.

"I want to," he said quietly.

She shrugged. "Middle drawer on your left. You'll find aprons and towels."

They worked silently for a few moments, then Mike asked, "Why in heaven's name are we doing this? What's the dishwasher for?"

171

Darcy gave him a shocked look. "For expensive china and crystal and silver?" She shuddered at the thought of water spots or soap film.

Mike chuckled. "Shows how much I know, doesn't it? You act like I committed a sacrilege." He stopped drying the cup in his hand and turned to look at her. "I can't tell you how proud I was of you tonight, Peanut. I wouldn't have blamed you for cancelling this morning when Maria came down sick. Yet you cooked a perfect meal and made a wonderful hostess. And now here you are, close on midnight, washing the dishes."

She looked back at him soberly. His words, which she knew could have thrilled her under other circumstances, left her cold. They meant less than nothing. Because all she could think of were Maxine's parting words to Mike. Neither of them had realised they were overheard. "I'll expect you Monday, then, Mike," she had told him softly as her scarlet-tipped fingers had clutched lightly at his sleeve. And Mike's head had bent towards hers so intimately. Now Darcy's heart felt heavy as a stone. She shrugged indifferently. "It's all just part of my job," she said. "The job I was hired to do."

Mike's eyes blazed angrily. "Is *that* how you look at it?"

She nodded, compressing her lips tightly. "Of course."

He flung down the tea towel, tore off the apron and whirled towards the door. "Then I'll leave you to it," he said in a harsh voice.

Darcy's shoulders hunched tiredly when he left. Her heart was pounding and she was close to tears.

It was after one before she managed to crawl wearily into bed. As miserable as she was, she expected to lie awake half the night, but exhaustion soon overtook her and she was swept off into a dreamless slumber.

She awoke as abruptly as she had fallen asleep, aware that something was wrong. And then she heard a cry coming from Kenny's room. Wide awake now, she stumbled out of bed, slid into the warmth of a long, white robe and hurried across the hall.

"What's wrong, love?" she asked softly as she turned on a lamp. She went to the crib and leaned over to touch him. He felt just a tiny bit warm.

She changed his diaper, got the liquid baby aspirin and managed to get him to take some. Then she picked him up, wrapped a blanket around him and sat down in the rocker.

He cried again even as he leaned his little head confidently against her breasts. "Me hurt," he complained. "Me hurt."

"We'll make it all better," she assured him. She kissed the top of his head and began rocking.

Mike appeared suddenly in the doorway, his dark hair tousled, a dark blue robe tied over his pyjamas. "I heard him cry," he said quietly as he entered the room. "What's wrong?"

"He's a little feverish," she told him.

"Do you suppose he's got the 'flu like Maria?"

"Probably."

"Is there anything I can do?"

Darcy started to shake her head, then nodded instead. "Would you fill a bottle with orange juice for him? I've been weaning him from his night-time bottle, but I really think it might help tonight."

He nodded and went out. Darcy crooned to the child nestled in her arms and it seemed to quieten him a little.

Mike returned with the baby bottle and Darcy scarcely noticed as he vanished again. She was too intent on watching Kenny.

He sucked thirstily at his bottle and sighed several times. Mike came back with two cups in his hands. "Hot chocolate," he said when she looked up enquiringly. "I thought you could use some."

"Thank you," she said huskily, touched at his thoughtfulness. He sat down in the other chair near hers and waited with her in the dim light as she rocked Kenny gently until his eyelids finally began to flutter and drop.

At last he gave a convulsive shudder, another sigh, and was deep in sleep. Mike came at once and took Kenny from her arms. She stood and watched quietly as he tenderly tucked the child back in his crib. Then he turned, touched her arm and guided her back to her own room.

She expected him to leave at once but instead, wordlessly, he removed her robe and tucked her into bed, too. She quivered, vulnerable to such thoughtfulness tonight. Her eyes were large as she looked up at him.

He sat down on the edge of the bed and took her hands tightly into his. "You've had a long day and a long night," he said softly. "You sleep in as long as you want tomorrow. I'll look after Kenny." And before she could speak, his head was bent close and his lips claimed hers.

If she had not been so tired, her brain so befuddled, she was certain she would never have responded as she did. But as his hands slid beneath her, lifting her against his warm chest, her arms seemed to move of their own volition up and around his neck.

The action seemed to inflame him and at once the gentle kiss turned into a strong, passionate demand. All at once he was lying beside her, and she could feel the hard, demanding maleness of his body pressed against hers. His hand slid inside her gown to cup her breast and fire streaked through her. His other hand moved down to her hips and pressed her closer to him. He kissed her hungrily, greedily — her eyes, her face, her hair.

But when he made a move to lift her gown, her reeling senses returned. "No!" she gasped, shoving against his chest with her fists. "No!"

His eyes, deep dark pools of passion, seemed to have trouble focusing for a moment. Then he really looked at her. "No?" he demanded incredulously. "What the hell do you mean, no? We're married. You're my wife, remember? And you know you want me as much as I want you." He reached for her again, but she moved further away from him.

"That's not true!" she denied vehemently. A vision of him and Maxine close together tonight rose up to spur her on. "I — I might have got a bit . . . carried away," she stammered out, "but I don't want you to make — make love to me. Our marriage is only a business arrangement, remember? Only temporary."

His eyes narrowed now and he gave her a calculating look. "Would you like it to be more than a business arrangement? More than temporary?"

Dear God! Now he was tempting her — tempting her more than flesh and blood could stand. She fought against a strong wave of aching desire for him. How she would love just to be able to fling herself into his arms, to abandon the reserve, to be able to submerge herself in her need of him. But he was just taunting her. He wanted her now physically, but there was no question of his loving her. And she knew she just had not the strength to be made love to by him and then, in the end, go away whole — when the time came for him to marry Maxine.

"No!" She was sobbing now into trembling hands. "No! No! No!"

He got up and stood looking down at her furiously. "Don't cry," he said harshly. "You're safe. I'm damned if I want an unwilling woman — even if she is my wife!" Angrily he stalked out of the room, leaving Darcy alone with her despair.

10

SUNLIGHT streamed through the open window into her face. She opened her eyes and watched tiny flecks of dust dancing in the shafts of light. "Darcy! Please, wake up!" Mike's voice sounded urgently in her ear. His hand shook her shoulder roughly.

She flipped over, staring up at him in amazement. Why was he here in her bedroom after their quarrel of the night?

But almost at once she realised something was badly wrong. A worried frown knitted his thick eyebrows together over his nose. Whatever Mike's reasons for being here now they had nothing to do with what had gone before. She raised herself up on an elbow and asked sharply, "What's the matter?"

"I brought you some coffee," he said, indicating the cup on the nightstand. "After you drink it, would you mind coming to look at Kenny? He seems

179

worse this morning and I don't know what to do."

Darcy sprang out of bed, heedless of appearing before Mike in only her sheer nightgown. In fact, she never even gave it a thought. She rushed past him across the hall into Kenny's room.

His breathing was raspy, laboured. Darcy reached over the crib rails and touched his unnaturally red cheeks. "He's burning up with fever!" she gasped. "Get the thermometer, Mike. It's in the medicine chest in my bathroom."

Mike was gone only a minute. When he returned, Darcy anxiously took Kenny's temperature. She staggered back disbelievingly when she read it. "One hundred and five!" She turned to look up at Mike with large, frightened eyes. "We've got to get him to a doctor at once!"

He nodded curtly. "Get dressed. When you get back, then I'll dress. Hurry!" Anxiety harshened his voice.

Darcy dressed with fumbling fingers. Bra, slip, blouse, skirt. Her body operated automatically and followed the routine of dressing without any conscious thought on her part. She reached into the closet

180

for her shoes. In her haste, it took a full two minutes before she could pull out a matching pair. Then there were her hair and lipstick to attend to. She ran a brush through her hair quickly, sparing it scarcely a thought. Her mouth quivered as she attempted to apply lipstick. She looked around wildly, looking for her handbag, which was in the top of the closet. She grabbed it and rushed back to Kenny's room.

Mike nodded without comment and headed towards his bedroom. Darcy opened the chest by the window and pulled out clean pants and a shirt. She dressed Kenny quickly. He cried constantly. "Oh, poor baby!" she murmured softly, brokenly. "Oh, my poor baby!" She packed the diaper bag hastily and, by the time she was done, Mike was back, dressed in slacks and a short-sleeved white pullover shirt.

"Ready?" he asked tautly.

"Yes." She moved towards the crib, but Mike scooped Kenny up himself and deftly tucked a blanket around him. The child was shaking with chills. Darcy picked up the diaper bag and silently they walked out to the garage.

Darcy slid into the front seat and Mike placed the fretful Kenny in her arms. Then he hurried around, got into the driver's seat and, in an instant, was backing out the Buick.

"Is there a doctor in Venture?" she asked.

Mike shook his head. "Nearest place is Wilson City."

Darcy bit her lip in consternation as the car manoeuvred down the gravelled county road. Wilson City. It would take a whole hour to get to town, and then how long a wait would there be before a doctor could see him? She looked down anxiously at the child in her arms. Kenny was gasping for breath and Darcy stared at him anxiously. Was he going to die right here in her arms?

The car swung on to the main highway and Mike picked up speed, but not fast enough to suit Darcy. "Can't you go any faster?" she begged.

Mike shot her a look, then his gaze moved down to the child's face, took in at a glance his laboured breathing. Mike was already doing five over the speed limit, but without a word he stepped heavily on the pedal. The speedometer crept up. Sixty-five; seventy; seventy-five; eighty. Darcy breathed a little easier.

Even so the drive seemed interminable. They raced past the turn off to Venture, past miles of lonely range land. Wildflowers grew in profusion along the roadsides. Sunflowers, black-eyed Susans, buttercups, Indian blankets, primroses were all lifting their delicate faces to the warm sun, but Darcy gazed at them unseeingly.

Mike kept his eyes glued to the highway, but once he asked, "How is he?" He glanced at her quickly and her pale face, the dark anxiety in her eyes, answered him mutely. His jaw tightened and again he paid strict attention to the road.

At last they reached the town. Mike slowed the car and wove deftly in and out of the churchgoing Sunday morning traffic. Darcy glanced down at Kenny's face again. A vice squeezed at her heart and, closing her eyes, she silently prayed.

Mike drove straight to the hospital, which was a three-story sprawling yellow brick complex with a wide expanse of green lawn. He parked near the emergency entrance and once again took Kenny into his arms. Darcy grabbed handbag and diaper bag and followed almost at a run, for Mike's long legs were striding widely across the cement drive.

A nurse sat at a reception desk. "May I help you?"

"We've got a very ill child here," he told her quietly.

"Do you have a local doctor, sir?"

"Len Bascom."

"I'll call him right away."

They had to sit in the waiting room for a few minutes while the nurse located Dr Bascom. But luckily the wait wasn't long because Dr Bascom happened already to be at the hospital making his morning rounds.

Darcy and Mike were escorted into an examining room where Dr Bascom joined them. "Hello, Mike," he greeted as he entered. "What's the problem?"

"It's Kenny, Len." He indicated the child on the examining table. Darcy was bent over him. "And this is my wife."

"Glad to meet you, Mrs Trent. Heard through the grapevine that Mike had married." He came to stand on the opposite side of the table. "Now, can you tell me his symptoms?"

"He can't breathe properly, Doctor," she told him quickly. "And his temperature is a hundred and five."

"Hmm." Dr Bascom reached for his stethoscope and bent over Kenny. "It's all right, son," he smiled. "We'll fix you up in no time."

A few moments later he stood back, looked first at Darcy, then at Mike. "Pneumonia," he said without preamble. "I think we'd better admit him to the hospital, Mike. We'll get him started on antibiotics at once, and I want to get him into an oxygen tent as fast as I can."

Darcy twisted her hands nervously. Mike nodded at the doctor. "I'll go sign him in now."

A few minutes later they were in the elevator, then walking down a long, bleak green-walled hall to the room which had been allotted to Kenny.

Luckily Darcy had packed him a pair of clean pyjamas. Now she undressed him and got him into them. A nurse came and gave him a shot which made him start crying again. Darcy held him close to her, trying to give him comfort. She looked up and met

Mike's eyes. His face was pale and grave.

Attendants came with an oxygen tent. Darcy had to put Kenny in the crib, while a nurse set up the apparatus. To Darcy, Kenny looked so distant with that cover over him. He looked so tiny and frightened. Darcy stood beside the crib, smiling down at him, trying to reassure him.

The nurse left and Mike came to stand beside her. His hand touched her shoulder and he squeezed it encouragingly, though neither of them spoke.

It was a long day. They both stayed at Kenny's bedside, afraid to leave him for an instant.

Around two that afternoon, a young volunteer girl in a pink and white striped dress came in and asked if they wanted anything from the coffee trolley. Mike bought two coffees, asked Darcy if she wanted a magazine and, when she shook her head, the girl went away again.

Periodically a nurse came and checked Kenny. Once she gave him another shot, then with a non-committal expression on her face, left the room briskly.

He slept a great deal — Darcy supposed it was the medicine which was making him so drowsy. She watched Mike walk over to the windows, look out, reach for a cigarette, remember, and put it back in the pack again.

The ugly scene between them the night before might never have been. Darcy was grateful for Mike's presence, his calm, quiet strength. Without him she was sure she would have fallen to pieces.

Once she asked him if he should not try to contact Don. He shook his head. "I talked with Len about it. Even if Don caught the first plane out he couldn't possibly get here before the day after tomorrow, and Len says the crisis will probably be over by then. He suggested we wait until morning and see how Kenny is then. If he's no better then I'll try to reach Don anyway." He rubbed his hand through his thick dark hair agitatedly. "Dear God! I hope it's the right decision."

She reached over and touched his hand in a spontaneous gesture. "It is," she assured him firmly. "It has to be. He's *got* to get well, Mike." She had been saying that over and over again in her mind, trying to convince herself of it. His eyes met hers and briefly his other strong, brown hand covered hers. Then they drew apart.

Around six o'clock Mike remembered that neither of them had eaten a thing all day. "I'll go down to the snack bar and pick us up a couple of hamburgers."

"I'm not hungry."

"Nevertheless, you have to eat," he said gently. "You can't let yourself get sick, too."

She supposed he was right and, when he returned, she forced herself to eat, though the food seemed just so much sawdust in her mouth. She thought fleetingly of the elegant meal she had served the previous night and of the dress she had worn. Tonight was light years away from last night. Tonight was tasteless hamburger, wrinkled clothes and nervous exhaustion.

Around ten an orderly wheeled in a bed, and Darcy looked at Mike quizzically. "For you," he said.

She did not speak until the orderly had made up the bed and gone away. "And where will you sleep, Mike? Are you going home?" A tiny, frightened note crept into her voice.

"Of course not. I'll either doze in a chair here or on the solarium."

"But you can't get any rest that way," she protested. "Why don't you take the bed and I'll — "

"Don't argue," he said wearily, as though he were dealing with a particularly unreasonable child and his patience had run thin, "You had a long hard day yesterday and another today. If you don't get some rest soon, you'll collapse."

Even so, she got little rest during the night. She was too keyed up, too nervous, too worried about Kenny. About every half hour or so she got up to check on him.

Towards dawn she decided it was senseless to try to sleep any more. She got up and washed her face in the basin, brushed her hair and tried to push the wrinkles out of her skirt. It was a hopeless situation.

Mike came in a few minutes later. "I thought you'd probably be up," he said softly. "Here, I brought you some coffee and doughnuts."

"Thanks." She sipped at the hot coffee and then looked up at him. His eyes were bleary from lack of sleep and his chin was dark with the stubble of a beard. His clothes, too, she noticed, were as limp and crumpled as her own. He

189

noted her appraisal and rubbed his hand over his chin, making a raspy sound. "What Kenny calls my cactus," he quipped. "We're neither of us candidates for the best dressed award today, are we?" Then he sobered and asked quietly, "How do you think he is?"

Darcy shook her head. "I don't know. His skin doesn't feel quite so hot, so his fever must be much lower, but his breathing . . . " She shrugged. "I just don't know. What time do you think the doctor will come?"

"A nurse told me probably between eight and ten. We'll just have to sweat it out until then."

It seemed a long time before Dr Bascom arrived, and when he did, they both rose and watched him anxiously as he examined the child. Then, before turning to them, he spoke in a low voice to the nurse.

"He's responding well to the medication," he said, smiling. "I think we'll take away the oxygen tent. Today we'll be sending him a lot of juices, Mrs Trent. Try to get as much down him as you can."

She nodded and he looked at them

both critically. "Have either of you had any rest?"

Mike shrugged. "A little, I guess. But really we've been too worried."

Dr Bascom nodded. "I thought as much." He turned to speak to the nurse again. "Mrs Clark, will you stay with Kenny for about half an hour or so while these two go down and get some breakfast? They're both about ready to drop."

The nurse smilingly agreed and, when Darcy would have protested, the doctor hustled her from the room.

They ate breakfast in the snack bar and then Mike led her to the solarium, where they could look out on a peaceful, green garden. "We'll stay here a few minutes," he told her. "You need a change of scenery."

She nodded dully, and without knowing she was about to, burst into tears. Mike came and pulled her into his arms. She squirmed, trying to back away, but he held her tighter. "Just get it all out of your system," he said softly.

Darcy stopped struggling. The broad, warm chest was so strong, so comforting as she rested her head wearily against it. She felt she wanted to stay there for the rest of her life. But finally the storm was over and she pulled away from him slowly. He handed her a large man-sized handkerchief and she dried her eyes. Peeping up at him apologetically through glittering, wet lashes, she whispered shakily, "I'm sorry — I don't usually cry. I can't think why I did."

"You've been under a big strain." He looked at her rather oddly and asked, "Does Kenny really mean that much to you?" The question was gentle and she found herself responding openly.

"Yes." Her voice was a mere whisper. "I was terrified he was going to die and I — I couldn't bear it." She looked up and met his eyes almost defiantly. "I love him, you see. Oh, I know he isn't mine, and that some day I'll have to let go of him, but — " She shook her head helplessly, unable to go on.

There was a strange glitter in his eyes. Their gazes locked, held, and Darcy felt almost paralysed. She couldn't have looked away just then. It would have been out of her power. In an oddly husky voice, he asked, "Do you want children of your own, Peanut?"

"Of — of course I do," she stammered. "Some day." Something within her made her boldly ask in return, "And you, Mike? Do you ever want children of your own?" Her voice cracked a little at the thought.

He looked down at her for a long moment, as though he were trying to read her very soul. Still she could not move, could not look away, could not break the spell. He nodded slowly and his voice had a strange little catch in it. "Do I want children? Absolutely."

A nurse came out just at that moment, pushing an elderly man in a wheelchair. The strange spell was broken; the oddly intimate moment gone. Mike was touching her arm impersonally now, suggesting, "Perhaps it's time we returned to Kenny."

Mike drove back to the Triple T that afternoon, long enough to bathe and change and have Maria pack Darcy a few clothes.

He returned around seven. "How is he?" he asked as soon as he entered.

"He seems much better." She smiled. "At least by comparison to yesterday."

"Good." His nod was brief, business-like. "Then you can leave here with a good conscience."

"Leave?" She stared at him. "Are you mad, Michael Trent? I'm not going to leave Kenny."

"Yes," he contradicted firmly, "you are. I've rented you a motel room a couple of blocks away." She opened her mouth to argue, but he lifted a hand, forestalling her. "You've got to have a place to bathe and change and get some sleep. Now I'll stay here with Kenny tonight. You can come back tomorrow morning and I'll head for home for a few hours' sleep and maybe get in a little work. Then I'll be back by dark. We'll work it that way."

Reluctantly, she agreed to do what he said. It would not have been any use to argue when he was this determined. She had learned that much about Mike Trent by now.

On Wednesday Kenny was much better, though he was still very weak and shaky. Darcy spent a lot of his waking hours rocking him gently, reading him picture books or simply singing to him softly. But the hours hung heavy on her hands. Each morning at six she returned to the hospital from the motel. Mike would leave immediately for the ranch, not returning

194

until six or seven in the evening. So, that afternoon, she was really pleased when Mrs Langley walked in.

"I would have been here sooner, my dear, but I only found out last night." She walked over to the crib and looked down on the sleeping Kenny. "How is he?"

"Much better. Dr Bascom says we can probably take him home by Friday or Saturday."

Mrs Langley nodded and sat down in the spare chair. Her grey hair was sleek and smooth, her navy suit dress neat and prim. Darcy felt grubby just looking at her. It was so hard to stay neat in a hospital, especially holding Kenny in her lap as much as she had. Now the older lady picked up a canvas bag beside her. "I stopped by the ranch first to see if I could bring anything you needed. Maria said you already had enough clothes, but I did bring you this." She held up a piece of Darcy's needlepoint.

"Oh, marvellous!" Darcy laughed. "You have no idea how the hours here drag."

"I thought it might help pass the time for you," Mrs Langley smiled. She picked up a gaily gift-wrapped package. "I also brought a stuffed monkey for Kenny."

"Thank you," Darcy said warmly. "How is Maria getting on?" she asked now. "She was ill herself when we left, and somehow I've just forgotten to ask Mike."

Mrs Langley's eyes twinkled. "Well, she had her hands full when I arrived. Maxine was there demanding to see Mike, but as he was sleeping, Maria absolutely refused to call him. She was very indignant that Maxine expected her to."

Darcy's throat suddenly felt dry. "Why did she want to see him so particularly?"

Mrs Langley laughed. "She *said* he was supposed to have come over to look at one of her cutting horses on Monday, with a view to buying. Anyway, Mike didn't show up or call. She hadn't heard about Kenny, of course, and she was absolutely livid over being stood up."

Darcy's face was taut. Now she bent over the canvas bag, drawing out her work, avoiding Mrs Langley's gaze. "I imagine Mike will apologise to her and smooth it over. He wouldn't have forgotten about her if he hadn't been so worried about Kenny."

"Of course," the older woman agreed

blandly. "But if you'll take my advice, you'll see to it he forgets her completely, cutting horses or no. Maxine is a very determined young woman."

Darcy met her look squarely. "I know."

Mrs Langley stood up to go. "And you," she added, "are the perfect wife for Mike, and I'm sure he realises that, else he wouldn't have married you." She paused and looked at Darcy thoughtfully. "Don't let someone like Maxine throw sand in the works, Darcy. It would be a tragic mistake to allow it."

But Darcy knew differently. Did Mike not allow Maxine more than her fair share of attention whenever she happened to be around? Mrs Langley only saw the surface appearances. She had no idea that Darcy's marriage to Mike was a business deal and that it was never supposed to be a real marriage at all — that it was never meant to last.

Mike fetched them and carried them home on Saturday. He was in a good mood and he chatted with Kenny, teasing him over a surprise he had waiting for him at home. Kenny did not exactly bounce on the seat between them, but his little face glowed with eager anticipation. He was happy to be going home at last, and so, Darcy thought with surprise, was she. Not that it was home, but because she thought of it as home. The Triple T was such a wonderful place for home to be.

"I've got a surprise for you too, Peanut," said Mike, cutting into her thoughts.

"Me?" She glanced up, flustered all at once.

Mike grinned. "But you get it only if you, like Kenny, promise to hug my neck."

"Oh!" He laughed at the dismayed expression on her reddened face and then answered some question of Kenny's.

Kenny's surprise was an adorable brown puppy that immediately proceeded to lick his face. Kenny hugged the squirming little body to him, and squealed with delight.

Mike touched Darcy's arm. "He won't even know we're around for a while. Come into the study, I want to give you your surprise."

She followed slowly, those words, 'hug my neck' still ringing in her ear. She was not sure how to cope with Mike in this teasing mood.

He picked up a black box and snapped

it open. Inside lay a beautiful bracelet, emerald and diamond-studded. It lay winking up at her provocatively.

When she did not say anything, Mike finally said flatly, "Let me put it on for you."

Darcy snatched both arms away from him, putting them behind her back. "No!" Her breath came hard, laboured, as though she had been running. She was blazingly angry. "You bought it because I stayed with Kenny, didn't you? As a payment for services rendered beyond the call of duty? How can you *dare* to attempt to put a price on what I did? You can't put a price on love!"

His face darkened and his eyes held murky depths. "If that's what you think I was doing, then the damn thing can go in the trash!" He slammed the box closed and proceeded to hurl it into the waste paper basket beside his desk. "That's obviously what your opinion is of me." Without another word, he strode from the room, leaving her staring blankly at the spot where he had stood.

11

THE front door slammed shut and she knew Mike had left the house. She stood frozen for another long moment and then she flung herself to the floor. Her hands trembled as she pulled the box out of the waste paper basket and hurried with it to her room, where she sank down on the bed and slowly opened the box. The lovely stones lay on a bed of white satin, glittering and catching prisms of light. She had never seen a more beautiful bracelet in her life.

Her head ached with confusion. Mike had been so furious at her refusal to accept it. Obviously she had misjudged his motives for giving it to her and she realised she must have hurt him badly. She knew now that she had spoken too precipitately, ravaged as she was by love and jealousy. But what reason could he possibly have had for giving the bracelet to her other than the reason she believed. She could not think that it was because he really cared for her. In the past, he had desired her physically, but never at any time had he shown that he felt anything more for her than that.

She raised a shaking hand to her throbbing temples. He had looked so obviously surprised — and then so blazingly angry. Had she gone beyond the lines of forgiveness with her curt refusal of his gift? He had obviously expected her to be pleased, and now she had ruined his wonderful surprise. She could only hope that it was not too late to make it up with him.

When she took her evening bath, she practised her apology. She would be humbly repentant and he would graciously accept her apology and everything would be fine between them again. There would be no more strain or strife.

She dressed carefully that night in a long white skirt with an emerald green blouse. Last of all she clasped the bracelet around her slender wrist. It glowed and winked magnificently in the mirror, and Darcy wet her lips and smiled at her reflection. "We're going to make the most of this evening, my girl," she told herself cheerfully.

While Maria put the finishing touches to the dinner, Darcy tucked Kenny up in his bed and read him a goodnight story. He had been unhappy about parting with his new little friend, but Darcy assured him that the puppy would be fine in the basket they had fixed up for him in the garage.

She kissed him warmly and Kenny's little arms crept up around her neck and hugged her to him. Tears stung Darcy's eyes. She would never ask anything more of this world than to be allowed to live here the rest of her life, loving Mike, making a home for him, a home for Kenny as well if his father allowed, a home — dare she think it! — for children of their own.

She forced herself to stop thinking this way. Just because she planned to make it up with Mike tonight it did not mean that anything basically would be changed. But even though she was afraid that it would never be anything more, she longed at least to be friends with him again. She did not want ever to see the look on his face again which she had seen this afternoon.

By seven-thirty Mike still had not come home, so Darcy went out to the kitchen and told Maria to go on home. "Mr Mike is a bit late and I don't know how much later he'll be. I'll do the washing up myself."

Maria acquiesced gratefully. "Thank you, Miz Trent. Felix and I are supposed to go to a dance tonight." Her smooth brown face glowed with anticipation.

Darcy smiled. "Well, you just go and have fun. If I'd known that I'd have sent you home earlier. You must tell me," she said reproachfully, "when you need to leave early."

"Oh, I didn't need to leave early," Maria answered. "The dance doesn't start until nine. I have plenty of time yet to dress."

Darcy waved goodbye to her as she left and then she returned to the family room. The house was so quiet. Kenny was already asleep; Maria was gone, Mike not yet home. Every little noise seemed magnified. She could hear the wind rustling the leaves on the live oak tree out front. She had put a porch swing on the patio, and now the chains squeaked as the wind rocked it gently. She could hear the ticking of the clock on the shelf, and from a distance she could hear the plaintive whines of the puppy in the garage.

She wondered what was keeping Mike.

Was he staying away because he was still angry with her, or because he was really busy? She sighed. She had no way of knowing and there was no answer in the clock's hands as they kept slowly moving around.

Finally she switched on the television, to distract her attention from the clock, but she soon turned it off again. She was too nervous tonight to get wrapped up in a detective show. She picked up her needlepoint and made two or three stitches, but the handwork did not soothe her tonight. She put it aside and then flipped through a magazine, but soon threw it down, and headed purposefully to the kitchen. Maria had left the dinner warm on the stove, but it had long since grown cold. Darcy had no appetite anyway, so she put the food away in the refrigerator. After all, it was close on eleven now. Surely Mike would not want food if he came in as late as this. She was perfectly certain he would already have eaten somewhere before now, while she had sat around waiting, hoping, listening.

She did the dishes listlessly, went in to check on Kenny again and then went into her own room. She took off the bracelet and placed it back in its black box. It lay winking at her, teasing, a symbol of all her unhappiness, of shattered dreams. She blinked back tears, refusing them the comfort of release as she undressed and crawled unhappily into bed.

It was a long time before she fell asleep, and Mike still had not come home when she finally dozed off fretfully.

The next morning he was gone before she awoke. At first she believed he had not come home all night, and began to get frightened, but when she looked inside his bedroom she saw that the bed was unmade. He had come home some time after she had gone to sleep.

It was a wretched morning. She was miserably certain now that he had been with Maxine last night. She had driven him to her with her cruel refusal of his generous gift. And who, she flayed herself bitterly, could blame him? Any man who offers his wife such a gift expects thanks and not a figurative slap in the face.

She went outside to work her flower beds, hoping that it would soothe her brooding thoughts. The hot July sun beat down upon her back as she bent over, loosening the soil with a trowel. But inside, she felt cold and frightened.

A truck pulled up and stopped in the drive. Darcy looked round eagerly, hoping it was Mike. A light gleamed in her eyes, a smile began on her parted lips.

But the light died and the smile became a forced one as she watched Vince Kirby walk towards her. She had not seen him since the night she had given the dinner party. Indeed, she had not thought of him once during this past week.

"Morning," he greeted her. His smile was warm and soft, and Darcy stirred, feeling uncomfortable as she remembered the words he had spoken to her that night.

"Good morning." She rose to her feet. "Have you come to see Mike about some business, because I . . . "

He shook his head. "I ran into him along the road. He sent me for you."

"Sent you? But why?"

He watched her closely. "He asked me to take you over to my place for the day. You haven't seen my home yet, you know."

"But why?" she demanded again. She

suspected he was making all this up just to lure her over to his house. Scepticism glowed in her eyes.

"Mike thinks you need to get out for a break. He said you've stayed cooped up with Kenny in the hospital all week and that you need a change before you break down and get sick yourself." That, definitely, sounded like Mike. Doubts that he had said it flew, but were replaced instantly with more doubts. Before, Mike had ordered her to stay away from Vince, yet now he was trying to throw them together. It did not make sense. It did not . . . Her eyes widened. Yes, it did make sense. Mike must be making it plain to her that he was through pretending, that he simply did not care any more, and what easier way to discard her than to hand her over to Vince, who was so obviously interested? A sharp pain slashed through her at the thought.

She lowered her head slightly and looked at the ground. "I see. Well thank you, Vince, but I don't think . . ."

"I promise you," he cut in quietly, "that I won't try to touch you, or speak about my feelings for you. Because it simply wouldn't matter to you, would it? You're really in love with Mike, aren't you?"

She nodded mutely, unable to hide her feelings at this moment. The truth lay bare for him to see.

"And Mike?" he asked softly.

Darcy looked up then, an angry gleam in her eyes. "You know very well how Mike feels — you told me so yourself."

"You mean Maxine?"

"Of course I mean Maxine." Her shoulders hunched.

Vince nodded. "I know I thought so, and that she hopes so. But . . . " He looked thoughtful and far away. "I'm not sure any more."

"Well, I am," she snapped. "Now, let's forget it, shall we?"

She smiled up at him now. The brilliance of the smile was slightly forced, a little too dazzling to be true.

"Now, will you come?" he asked her, smiling with only frank friendliness in his eyes. "I thought you might like to go horseback riding after lunch."

Darcy nodded agreement this time. If Mike wanted her to go, she would go. The world went on regardless of one's wounds. One simply licked them and kept on moving.

She admired his home. It was a two-storey white brick with huge pillars in front, a far more formal and ostentatious house than Mike's. The interior was also completely formal and elegant, with gold and white trim throughout. Darcy thought it beautiful, but in the way one can admire a statue or a painting, yet knowing at the same time that it wouldn't be right for oneself. It was all too cold, too perfect, too unlived-in somehow, really to be a home.

They shared a pleasant luncheon which was served by Vince's manservant, Juan. The dining room was almost overpowering in its size and magnificence. A crystal chandelier hung above the long table and a huge mural of elegant ladies and gentlemen and horse-drawn carriages from days gone by decorated one wall. Darcy, in a simple skirt and blouse, felt as out of place as a palm tree at the North Pole.

After lunch, she changed into the jeans she had brought along and they walked down to the stables where two saddled horses awaited them.

The ride was enjoyable, but Darcy could

not help but compare it to the other one she had taken with Mike. There had been such a warm, friendly bond between them that day.

She tried hard to keep up a happy front for Vince. She had no right to inflict her unhappiness on someone else, and though she had broken down before him briefly, her pride had reasserted itself and now she desperately wished to erase that scene from his mind.

It was almost five when Vince drove her back home. As he pulled to a stop in the drive, he turned to her and smiled. "See! That wasn't so bad, was it?"

"It was wonderful," she told him, suddenly struck by the realisation that he must be hurting inside, too. He had told her that night that he loved her, but today, after her damning admission of her love for Mike, he had been casually friendly, not hinting once of his own emotions. Life was so unfair, she thought sadly. Why couldn't she have fallen in love with Vince? How easy everything would have fallen into place, then. Nobody would be getting hurt. But she knew that however kind and friendly and likeable Vince was, she could never love him. Her heart had been stormed by a stranger's kiss, the first time she had ever seen Mike, that day he had saved her life.

"If you ever need me, Darcy," Vince was saying now, awkwardly, "I mean — well, if things don't work out and you — Well, if you ever change your mind, let me know. I'll be waiting."

Tears stung her eyes and she blinked hard. Impulsively, she placed her hand over his for a moment. "Thank you, Vince," she said huskily. "But, no matter what happens, I can never change my mind."

He nodded soberly. "I know. But I'll go on hoping anyway."

Darcy bathed and dressed listlessly for dinner that evening. Completely gone was the hope and eager anticipation of the night before. Mike was obviously avoiding her, so once again he probably would not show up until late tonight. She did not wear the bracelet; she could not even bring herself to look at it again. The whole matter was too painful.

She was a little pale as she went towards the family room. She was preparing herself for another long evening alone.

But Mike stood beside the fireplace when she entered, staring down at a bowl of gay zinnias and marigolds set in the hearth. He lifted his hand to take another sip of his drink when he suddenly saw her. His face was grave, his dark eyes two black coals as he looked at her.

"Did you have a nice day with Vince?" he asked abruptly.

"Yes. He told me you asked him to invite me." When Mike did not answer, she asked, "Why? The night I met him you told me to stay away from him."

He shrugged and took a long swallow of his drink. She still looked at him questioningly and now he said irritably, "Does it matter?"

"I think it does," she said quietly.

"Let's just say that I changed my mind. He's certainly eager for your company and you seem to enjoy his better than mine, so — " He shrugged again. "Why not?"

She moved closer to him, ignoring his last words. "Mike, I — " She licked her dry lips and swallowed over a lump in her throat. "I want to apologise about yesterday. I'd like to thank you for the bracelet."

212

His eyes narrowed. "So! You fished it out, then?"

"Yes."

He laughed harshly, but there was no humour in it. Sarcastically he sneered, "I thought you would. It's worth a considerable amount. Girls don't usually throw away expensive jewels."

Her hand shot out to touch his arm appealingly. "Mike!" Her mouth trembled. "Please, don't be that way."

His eyebrows lifted. "What way?" His eyes took on an inscrutable look. He raised his arm again, to take another drink from the glass he held, effectively loosening her touch from his sleeve. "The point is, my dear little wife, your thanks come just a bit late after throwing the gift back in my face like you did."

"But Mike, I simply didn't understand your motives. I'm sorry." She had to break through his barrier of aloofness. She simply had to.

He looked down at her derisively. "And you understand what my motives were now?"

Colour came and went in her cheeks. "No," she said slowly, "I guess not."

He moved away from her towards the bar and set his empty glass down on its polished surface. "And I'm damned well not going to explain them to you, either."

They got through dinner somehow, though afterwards, Darcy could not remember a word they had said at the table. She only knew that they had spoken politely and on indifferent subjects whenever Maria was in the room, but when she was out, they had immediately lapsed into a brooding silence. The situation between them now seemed hopeless.

Immediately after dinner Mike excused himself with frigid politeness and, a few moments afterwards, Darcy heard the car roar down the driveway. She wondered if he was going to Maxine again. Her entire body hurt with the thought as she moved down the hall to her bedroom.

The black box lay mockingly on her dresser. Instead of accepting her apology and her thanks, Mike now believed she had taken the bracelet after all because of its monetary value. Under no circumstances could she keep it now, not with him believing the worst of her as he did.

She picked up the box and went into

Mike's room. He had tossed his straw everyday work hat on to a chair. She bent down and picked it up, holding it against her. Why had everything turned so wrong? She gripped the hat tightly, as though by its very touch she could wring out an answer to her question.

Finally she dropped it back on to the chair. She moved across to the bureau and opened the top drawer, about to deposit the bracelet there.

But her action was halted by shock and disbelief and wonder. She pulled out the large, framed photograph. When had he had this done, she wondered. And why? It was an enlargement of the best of the pictures Slim had taken of them together that day. In the picture she was smiling, Mike laughing, and his arm was around her shoulders, her blonde hair against his broad chest, a contrast to his darkly tanned face.

Having a photograph enlarged and carefully framed was something not thoughtlessly done. A person did such a thing deliberately or it was not done at all. So why had Mike done this? Was it for the same inexplicable reason that he had presented her with the bracelet?

She replaced the photograph carefully, slammed shut the drawer, picked up the black box and returned to her room. Her heart sang crazily and she smiled to herself. Maybe Mike did not love her, but he must care for her in some way. Else why the photo — why the gift? Tonight he had been coldly aloof and had made it plain he did not want any part of her. But was that only a defence? Darcy made up her mind to one thing alone as she undressed for bed. She loved Mike, and until she had positive proof that that picture and that bracelet did not mean he cared for her at all, she was going to act on the assumption that they did. She would shed her pride, her reserve, and let him see as openly as she dared that she loved him. Maybe — just maybe — then the miracle would happen.

She went to bed in a hazy fog, weaving fantastic dreams, and thinking the most loving of thoughts about the man who had married her. She recalled the times he had held her in his arms and kissed her. If only she could be given another chance, Mike would be shocked at how differently she would respond.

She awoke abruptly the following morning. The sun was bright in her eyes. Why was it so bright? She twisted over to look at her bedside clock. Eight-fifteen! She could not believe it! She usually awoke at five in order to make coffee and cook Mike's breakfast! How could she have let this happen — when she had wanted so much to be up with him for breakfast this morning at that peculiarly intimate time, the first beginning of day, before Maria arrived or Kenny awakened? And now she was too late! She could have cried with vexation.

She dressed quickly and hurried down the hall. Maria, of course, would already have fed and dressed Kenny, but she felt guilty about it, anyway. She could only suppose that her long week of constant vigil and worry at Kenny's bedside had finally caught up with her as a reason for oversleeping like this. A logical assumption, she supposed, but she still chaffed with annoyance.

The green drape panels were still drawn in the family room as she entered it, and she paused to pull them open. She did not like any part of the house to be darkened on a bright, sun-washed day.

Her eyes caught a flash of movement and suddenly she was transfixed. From where she was looking, she could see Mike and Maxine alighting from their horses at the barn. Mike handed the reins to Buck, who led them inside the barn, and then Mike and Maxine turned and began walking slowly towards the house. They were both smiling and Mike paused and bent down close to her as though to hear better something she was saying. Suddenly Maxine's arms went around Mike's neck and the two bodies were close together in the bright, blinding sunlight.

Darcy turned away, sick at heart. *Fool!* She told herself. *Fool ever to think you stood a chance. It's always been Maxine with him. And last night you had such high hopes! Fool!*

She clenched her hands tightly at her sides. *I don't love him!* she told herself. *I don't. I hate him! I hate him!*

12

A FEW minutes later, Darcy heard Mike calling her. "We have company!" he yelled. She had returned to her bedroom and now she clenched her fists into a tight knot and took in a deep breath. She straightened her shoulders and then returned to the family room she had just left.

She was cool and, at least, outwardly calm, by the time she joined them. She would never allow either of them to have the satisfaction of seeing how hurt she was. Now she smiled welcomingly. "Why, good morning," she greeted, simulating pleased surprise. "How nice to see you again, Maxine."

The other girl smiled archly up at Mike. "I've been having an early morning horseback ride with Mike, the way we used to do."

"That sounds very nice," Darcy said smoothly. "You must both be starved. Would you like some breakfast?"

"Well," Maxine looked becomingly hesitant, "I wouldn't want to put you out any."

"No trouble at all," Darcy smiled graciously. "I'll just tell Maria. We'll have it on the patio, it's so pleasant out there."

Mike forestalled her as she would have moved. "Never mind, I'll tell Maria for you. I can't stay. I had my breakfast early, so I'll just grab a cup of coffee." He walked towards the kitchen door.

Maxine looked irritated and Darcy hid her grim amusement. Maxine might command Mike's attention part of the time, but not all of it. He was shaking her off pretty fast now their ride was over. She was sure the other girl was already regretting her acceptance of breakfast, now that she knew it did not include Mike's company.

Politely, she invited Maxine out to the patio. It looked especially lovely this morning. The green ferns were like delicate lace fluttering gently in the slight breeze; the tall potted palms gave a lush, tropical atmosphere; red geraniums in clay pots provided a splash of colour.

They sat down at the wrought-iron

garden table. They could see Kenny playing contentedly with his puppy near the garage.

"Kenny still looks pale and ill," Maxine commented. "Shouldn't he be in bed instead of outside playing?"

"The doctor says not," Darcy responded. "As long as he gets sufficient rest, he advised letting him out for quiet play for a part of each day."

Maxine shrugged, then looked at Darcy keenly: "Don't think I'm being interfering, my dear." The 'my dear' came out patronisingly, and Darcy stiffened. "But are you sure you're really quite capable of taking care of such a young child?"

"What do you mean?"

Maxine shrugged again, delicately, with a half-smile on her lips. "Only that you've had no previous experience dealing with young children. And after all, he did come down with pneumonia. Perhaps if you'd watched his diet, his rest, his play a bit more carefully?" The question hung in the air between them.

"What exactly *are* you trying to say?" Darcy asked at last in a cold voice.

221

"Oh, I don't know exactly. This is so awkward, and I'm sure I'm saying it all wrong, but — well, you must know that Mike seems a bit concerned since Kenny got so ill. He wonders, you know, whether perhaps he made a mistake. After all, he is entrusted with Kenny's welfare. But," she added brightly, as though eager to soften the blow, "Mike did tell me how wonderfully you carried on while Kenny was in hospital."

Darcy never knew how she got through the remainder of Maxine's visit. But she must have smiled at the right places, said the right things, because when Maxine finally did take herself away, she was smiling sweetly and suggesting another chummy shopping trip together some time soon.

Could Mike really have discussed her with Maxine? Pain drummed through her head. Something like a vice squeezed her heart. Could Mike have admitted to Maxine that he had made a mistake in marrying her, in giving Kenny over to her care?

She looked down and was amazed to see that her hands were trembling violently.

In fact, her entire body was chilled and shaking.

She would have to leave; there was no use pretending otherwise any longer. She could not possibly stay on for another year under these conditions. This morning her husband had gone riding with another woman whom later Darcy had seen him embrace. Then this same woman had come and expressed Mike's doubts about his marriage. Had Mike, Darcy wondered now for the first time, brought Maxine over so she could deliberately have a talk with her?

That thought brought waves of humiliation and a renewed determination to leave as soon as possible. Either at noon or tonight she would today force a conversation with Mike. She would tell him she wanted to go just as soon as they could find someone else to come and care for Kenny.

Kenny! She would miss him so much when she went away. She stood up determinedly and went to the bathroom, where she washed her face. She must go out and be with Kenny. Maria could run the house by herself. Darcy wanted to spend all her remaining time here being with the little boy, because those times would be the only good memories she would take away with her when she left the Triple T for good.

Emotion choked her as she played with Kenny and his puppy. Soon she would go away and never see his dear little face again, would never feel the velvety softness of his cheek pressed against hers; never see his winning smile or hear his laughter. It would be hard, once she was away somewhere all alone, to remember his exuberant company and know she would never see or hold him again.

Darcy steeled herself to confront Mike at noon about the matter. It was wasted effort, however, for when noon finally came, Mike did not. And just as she was about to sit down and eat her meal alone, Maria dropped a new blow. "Mr Mike said he wouldn't be home for supper tonight, ma'am. So do you want to change the menu, seeing it'll just be you to eat?"

Darcy stared at the Mexican girl blankly for a minute, scarcely able to take in the fact that Mike had told the servant, rather than herself, that he would not be home either for lunch or the evening meal! It seemed to be the final, bitter humiliation in a day of constant humiliation. Mike seemed to be making it very clear that, as far as he was concerned, he was through with her altogether.

Distractedly, she made some answer to Maria even as pain coursed through her body, leaving her feeling limp and weak.

She would have packed and left that very afternoon, without even seeing Mike, but Mrs Langley and several other church ladies dropped in for a visit, and by the time they left it was too late for Darcy herself to leave.

In all likelihood therefore she would see Mike in the morning. Well, so much the better. She had no real desire to sneak out and she would feel better about it if she could tell him that she was leaving. After all, he would have to make some plans about Kenny. Earlier, she had meant to give him notice and then stay until he found someone else to come and take care of Kenny, but that was now impossible. She felt she just could not stay any longer.

She lay awake for hours that night as the torturing memory of Maxine in Mike's arms that morning rose up to taunt her.

How was she ever going to forget Mike? Because as much as he had hurt her today, she still loved him, and she knew that the scars from that love would remain with her for the rest of her life. But the hurt, after all, was her own fault. Mike had never made any promise of love, had never made any promises of their marriage ever becoming permanent. He had been perfectly honest with her that day. He had told her that he needed her help, but nothing more. Because, though she had not known it then, Maxine stood by only too ready to give him all else that he needed. No, it was her own treacherous heart that was at fault. Rationally, she had known from the start that it would be dangerous to fall in love with Mike. Emotionally it had been impossible not to do.

She finally dropped off into a fretful, uneasy sleep in which she dreamed that Mike was saving her life from a car accident. Maxine was there in flowing white, and Mike offered Darcy some peanuts to eat before, with Maxine at his side, he rode away on a horse, leaving her alone.

She was awakened roughly. "Wake up! Kenny is crying for you!" A strong hand shook her shoulder violently.

She opened her eyes bemused, and looked up at Mike. Where were Maxine and the horses? she wondered in confusion. Mike's face was dark as he loomed above her. "Wake up! Can't you hear Kenny? He's awake and hungry. It's six o'clock. Don't you think you should get up and stick to your part of this marriage bargain?" His voice was harsh and brutal.

The dream faded; reality set in. Darcy slid out of bed, ran her fingers through her tousled hair, then reached for her robe at the same time as Mike. Their fingers met briefly and she jerked her hand away quickly as though she had been burned. Mike held the robe open, so that she had no choice but to slip her arms through the sleeves.

He looked at her grimly. "Don't you have any comment to make? I'm waiting for one of your famous retorts."

She whirled on him, then, furiously angry. "I want to end this — marriage bargain — as you call it. I want to end it now! Maria can look after Kenny until you find someone more suitable. And that shouldn't be too difficult for you, even if you did make a mistake about me."

"You'll do no such thing!" he snarled at her, slightly baring his teeth. "We made a bargain and you'll stick to it whether you like it or not!" Suddenly his arms reached out and pulled her against him, holding her tightly, so that she could scarcely breathe. His head bent and she read fury in the dark eyes a moment before his lips claimed hers.

It was a brutal kiss, insistent, demanding, hard. His hands pressed her hips against him and then one hand came around and moved insolently over her body which was still soft and warm from sleep. She tried to pull away from him and gasped for breath.

He released her abruptly and he stood glaring at her from narrowed eyes. "I told you once that I didn't want an unwilling woman even if she was my wife. But I've changed my mind. Tonight I intend to take what belongs to me." He walked towards the door and added grimly, "For the moment I think you'd better attend to the baby."

"I hate you!" she whispered in a choked voice. "Do you hear me? I hate you!"

He shrugged his shoulders indifferently. "So be it. Hate or love, you'll act like a real wife to me for the duration of our marriage."

"But why?" she demanded. "You can't really want me — I saw you yesterday kissing Maxine. So why are you doing this? To punish me?"

"I have no intention of discussing my reasons with you. Now — " he opened the door wide, "are you going to Kenny?"

Kenny stopped crying instantly when Darcy entered his room. She thrust her furious thoughts from her and cooed soothing words to him. By the time she had him out of his pyjamas and into his clothes, he was chuckling contentedly.

She dressed hurriedly in her own room, then rushed to the kitchen. Mike had made coffee and poured out two cups. He turned, picked up Kenny and put him in his high chair while Darcy began filling the skillet with sausage and breaking eggs into a bowl.

Mike kept up a running stream of nonsense with the child, but to Darcy he said nothing. For her part, she kept her eyes averted from him. Her mind was whirling with her own plans and she did not want Mike to guess. If he looked into her eyes, she was afraid he would know.

After Mike had eaten, he stood up and pulled on his hat. Then he looked soberly at her. "We seem to have been saying and doing a lot of things at cross-purposes lately, Peanut." It was the first time since Kenny's return from the hospital that he had called her by the old familiar name, and Darcy looked up at him in surprise, forgetting to shield her eyes. Even in his rough denim shirt, the faded levis, he was very good-looking. His face, bronzed from the sun, was almost as dark as the Mexican Americans who worked for him. Darcy found herself storing away Mike's image in her mind. His next words brought her back to alert attention. "Tonight I think we'd better hash it all out before bedtime."

She looked away as the colour in her face heightened. "I don't think there's anything to discuss," she said stiffly.

"You're wrong," he contradicted flatly. "We need to discuss Maxine — among other things."

She looked at him again, this time with stormy eyes. "The last thing you need

230

to discuss with me is your relationship with Maxine. This, at least, is quite clear to me!"

He lifted his eyebrows and looked at her humorously. "Is it now?" he drawled. "I intend to make it clearer still." He turned abruptly and went out the door.

Listlessly she began to scrape the dishes and load them in the dishwasher. If Mike intended to confront her tonight with his love for Maxine, that was something she could not face. She would be gone — she was determined on that point. There was everything to be gained by leaving and much to lose by staying. And the last thing she could bear was to hear Mike put into actual words his feelings for Maxine. Dear God, she must be spared that agony!

Maria came in the back door. "Is very foggy outside this morning. I had a hard time finding my way to the house."

"Really?" Darcy asked vaguely. She peered out of the window. A thick white cloud blocked a view of all but the patio, and it was only an indistinct blur. "It will clear up soon, I imagine, as soon as the sun burns it off." She poured herself a second cup of coffee. "I'm driving into town to do some shopping after lunch," she told the girl. "You'll watch Kenny closely for me, won't you?"

"*Si*," Maria smiled, and nodded. "*Si*, I'll take good care of him."

Darcy returned to her room. Packing would not take long because she intended to take only a few of the less expensive clothes with her. Mike had bought everything she owned, she thought, suddenly tearful. Everything. By rights she should go away with nothing, but that was not practical. She had to have some clothes, some money. When she reached Wilson City she would draw just enough cash from the bank to tide her over until she found a job and began earning money. Then she would be able to start paying Mike back. Because she would not be keeping their marriage bargain after all, her debt to him was not yet paid in full.

Dresses, slips, bras, a couple of nightgowns — Darcy folded the clothes quickly and deftly packed them into the small weekend bag. She wondered in bitter amusement what Mike would end up doing with the rest of her clothes. They were too small for Maria, but perhaps they could find someone who wore her size and needed items like a silver dinner dress.

A knot lodged in her throat and she had difficulty swallowing. The silver dress — she remembered how Mike had looked at her that evening before Maxine had arrived! She moved over to the closet and stood looking at it, stroking it. It was not likely that she would ever again in her life need a dress like that. In fact, it was not until she had become Mike's wife that she had ever needed them.

She had no clear-cut idea of where she should go. Should she go to Houston again? Or Austin? She thought longingly of Carolyn Lane. Should she go to her? No, she thought, that would not work. Mike would probably look there for her first of all. In her heart, she was very sure that Mike would look for her — not because he wanted her, she felt, but because he would not like being tricked or thwarted. The only way he would want her to go would be at his own bidding and in his own time, and in his own way. So where should she go? Corpus Christi? That would be too close. San Antonio? That also would be too near. She sighed. She planned to drive the Buick to Wilson City and leave it at the bus station. After she was safely away, she would either call or write Mike, telling him where to find his car. Perhaps the best idea would be simply to catch the first bus leaving town, and decide later where she wanted to stay.

With a snap she closed the bag, then looked around. There was the black jeweller's box on the dresser. Darcy picked it up and opened it for one last time. The bracelet was so lovely. What a gift it would make to a girl from the man who loved her! She blinked back tears. Yet Mike had thought she wanted it because of its value. She shut the box, reached in a drawer and brought out the pearls. She looked at them for a long time, and then her engagement and wedding rings. She touched them gently. They had never meant a thing — and oh, how she had prayed that some day they would symbolise a real marriage, a shared love.

She straightened her shoulders resolutely, picked up the jewellery and carried it all into Mike's room. Once more she opened the top bureau drawer. There was a neat stack of handkerchiefs on one side which she herself had pressed; on the other side was the framed photograph of Mike and herself together. She gave the photograph one last, quick glance and then gently placed the jeweller's boxes beside it. As she closed the drawer she had a vivid sensation of closing a door on her happiness. But that was ridiculous, she felt. There *was* no happiness for her to close a door on.

She waited until she heard the whirl of the vacuum cleaner, which told her that Maria was busy in the living room, before she carried her bag out to the garage and deposited it in the trunk of the Buick. By now the mist had burned off, leaving a clear, brilliant day. Darcy paused on the patio and gazed around longingly. In a few hours' time she would be gone and she would never see all this again — the corrals and pens in the distance, and beyond them, farther away still, the trees which shielded the creek. To her left and right were green pastures as far as she could see, sprinkled with placid, grazing cattle.

She listened to the hum of busy insects, and watched a small hummingbird dart between flowers near the house. She sucked in a deep breath of clean, pure air. Tears pricked at her eyelids and impatiently she brushed her hand across her eyes. This was no time to get sentimental. She should never have allowed herself to fall in love with Mike, with little Kenny, with this place. It was never meant to be her home.

Now she was in a fever to get away, impatient to leave. But she did not dare go before noon. Mike had not said he would be home for lunch, but neither had he said he would not. Not knowing the answer, Darcy did not dare leave yet. She had told him she wanted to leave, and if he came home at noon and found her gone, he would probably guess at once. But if she left after lunch, he would not be likely to know of it until nightfall and by then she hoped she would be many miles away from the Triple T. *Where* she went no longer mattered. It was only urgent that it be a place where Mike could never find her.

She spent the remainder of the morning playing with Kenny and his puppy. Together they all walked down the long gravel drive to the mail box. Darcy collected the envelopes, noticing that one was from Kenny's father. She looked down at Kenny's prancing little figure. The boy's colour was returning now and except for the fact that he still tired easily, he seemed completely recovered from his illness.

Now she had to give Kenny his lunch and tuck him up for his nap. He demanded a story and she told him the one about the Three Little Pigs. "Huff! Puff!" he repeated happily. "Blow house down!"

When she had finished, she kissed him and hugged him so hard that he squealed in protest. But he had no idea it was the only way she could say goodbye.

Mike did not show up at lunch time. Darcy felt impatient with herself. If she had taken a chance and left earlier, she would already have been miles away.

She only toyed with her lunch, her mind in a fever of turmoil, and as soon as she thought she could leave the table without arousing Maria's suspicions, she rushed to her room. She took a quick shower and dressed hurriedly in a cream slack suit with a printed brown blouse. Then she grabbed her handbag, shot a last look at her room and went out.

Her hands were fumbling as she put the key into the ignition, and stepped on the starter. She had not been aware that she had been holding her breath until she breathed out heavily as the motor spurted to life. Nothing must stop her now.

She drove down the driveway and around the curve — out of sight now from the house. She reached the mail box and pulled out on to the gravelled, rural road. In ten miles she would reach the main highway. She felt tense, knowing that there was still a thousand-to-one chance she might meet Mike on the road.

The road was rough. The big car bounced and jostled as though it had been a jeep. Darcy gritted her teeth, aware suddenly that the car was not driving as it ought. It should not be this rough — there was something wrong. She would have to stop.

She got out and walked around the car. The right rear tyre was as flat as the proverbial pancake.

Coming on top of all else that had happened recently, this was too much. Her lips quivered and, unable to hold herself in check any longer, she burst into tears.

A car pulled up in front of her and she turned away to hide her tears, but suddenly she was pulled into a pair of arms. "What is it, Darcy?" She recognised Vince Kirby's anxious voice. "Are you hurt?"

She shook her head, trying to get a grip on herself. "No. But I was leaving and now . . . I've got a flat tyre! Oh, Vince!" She lifted her wet lashes and looked at him appealingly. "Please help me . . . help me to get away. I've got to leave!"

"You're leaving Mike?" he asked in surprise.

She nodded.

"Does he know it?"

"No. He — he mustn't — Not until I've had time to get away. Please, help me!"

He looked at her thoughtfully and there was a tiny pucker between his eyes. "You know I love you, Darcy," he said at last, "and that I'd do anything I could for you. But are you sure you're doing the right thing by going like this?"

Before she could answer, a truck drew to a screeching stop behind them. A door slammed and, almost immediately, Darcy heard the voice she had dreaded.

"What in the hell," Mike demanded in a dangerously controlled voice, "do you think you're doing holding my wife in your arms?"

13

DARCY stiffened. Vince dropped his arms from her as though she were on fire and stepped backward. Mike's strong hand grabbed her wrist and she was jerked back against him. "What do you think you're doing?" he hissed.

"It — it wasn't what you think," she stammered, anxious to absolve Vince from any blame. Mike's face was like a black thundercloud and she shivered, suddenly afraid.

"Be quiet!" Vince ordered, and she glanced at him in surprise. His face, too, was dark with anger. He transferred his stormy gaze to Mike. "Darcy was crying because she needed to get away from you," he said bluntly, "and then she had a flat tyre. I found her crying and I just naturally put my arms around her. But if you care to make something more of it, I'm ready," he added belligerently. "It's always best to stay out of husband and wife quarrels, Trent, but I happen to love Darcy myself. It's clear you're nothing but a brute to her, and I'm damned if I'll stand by meekly and watch you bully her. She should never have married a man like you, and I intend to do everything in my power to help her get free of you."

Mike's eyelids narrowed over the murky depths of his eyes. "So that you can marry her yourself once she's free?" he asked harshly.

Vince nodded. "That's right."

Suddenly Darcy was thrust behind Mike. "Stay out of the way!" he ordered, even as he clenched his fists and moved slowly towards Vince in a crouched position. "Okay, Kirby, that's it. Nobody is going to stand there and tell me he's going to take my wife from me! What kind of a man do you think I am?"

Vince knotted his fists too, and moved forward. "I was hoping you were a man big enough to let go of a woman who doesn't want you."

Both of them must be stark, staring mad, thought Darcy. She looked around frantically, as though by magic someone, something, anything, would be conjured up which would put an end to this business. But there was only the blazingly hot sun beating down relentlessly upon her head, the fenced pastures bordering the road, a butterfly flitting unconcernedly by, the rustle of weeds in the slight breeze and the two men facing up to each other. She moved swiftly, without thinking, between them, her hands outspread and a cry of "Don't!" on her lips. A glancing blow struck her shoulder and she slumped with pain.

"Oh, my God!" Mike moved forward and caught her in his arms as she fell. "Peanut! Sweetheart! Are you all right? I never meant . . . "

The pain was lessening now and she shoved him away roughly, ignoring the tender, meaningless words, the anxious concern in his eyes. "You're both nothing but a couple of savages!" she spat furiously. "Fighting — as if I was that important! I don't know why you think it's necessary! You know what a fraud this whole marriage is, anyway!" She was too angry now to care any more about pretence. Then she turned on Vince, who was staring at her in hopeful amazement. "As for you — I told you there could never be anything between us! I intend to go away and I devoutly hope I never set eyes on either of you again! There never was any question of my marrying you! If you want to know the truth, I'm heartily sick of the word!" With that she stalked away to Mike's truck and got in on the passenger side.

Let the two idiots fight if they liked, she thought ferociously. Maybe it would knock some sense into their heads. As for herself, she still intended to leave. Maybe she could not today — not with a flat tyre and Mike on to her plans, but he could not keep her a prisoner. He would have to let her go after today.

She watched through the windshield as the two men talked a few minutes more. Their fighting mood was obviously now over, because a moment later they shook hands. Mike came back to the truck and climbed in beneath the steering wheel. She ignored him until he switched on the ignition. "Aren't you going to change the flat on the car?" she enquired coldly, not really caring.

He manoeuvred the truck into a turn on the narrow road. "I've got too much

243

else to do. I'll send one of the hands down to do it."

"I'm sorry I interrupted your busy schedule," she said sarcastically. "You really needn't have bothered about me."

"Think nothing of it," he rejoined. "A man must always be prepared to run down a troublesome wife."

She bit her lip. "Then you knew I was going?"

He nodded grimly.

"How?" she asked curiously. She had thought she had been so careful in her plans, not even daring to leave a note behind.

"I came up to the house right after you left, apparently — had to check some papers and make a phone call. Then I went to my room to get a clean handkerchief." As he said this he pulled out the handkerchief and wiped his wet face.

"I see." So he had seen the jewellery, the wedding and engagement rings, and drawn his own conclusions.

They were silent for the rest of the drive back to the house. Darcy kept her eyes glued painfully to the passing scene. She could see a yucca here, a prickly pear there, a few clumps of wildflowers mixed with the weeds that grew along the fence lines.

When the truck drew to a stop in the drive, Darcy finally looked at him. "So — what now?" she asked, somehow managing to get a flippant note into her voice.

Mike's face was stern and forbidding. "Now you go inside and stay put. I've got to get back to work. We'll talk this out tonight."

Darcy climbed down from the truck and gave the door a satisfying bang. She went towards the house, head held high, shoulders straight. Without a backward glance, she went inside.

Maria, who was busily polishing furniture in the family room, looked up in astonishment. "Miz Trent! I thought you left to go shopping!"

"Yes. Well, my car had a flat tyre." Darcy ran her fingers agitatedly through her hair.

"Oh, that's too bad!" the other girl said sympathetically. "Did you have to walk back?"

"No. Mr Mike came along and found me.

He brought me back." She moved towards the hall to avoid any more explanations. "That hot sun gave me a splitting headache, Maria. I think I'll go to my room and lie down for a while."

She went to her room, needing to escape from Maria's keen eyes, but she was too enraged to rest. She paced irritably back and forth. What incredibly bad luck she had experienced! It had been bad enough to have the puncture that prevented her from getting away undetected, but that Vince should come along and Mike find her in his arms was bordering on a comic farce.

She bit her lips so angrily that she drew a spurt of blood. She was not going to obey Mike's orders that she stay put, as though she was a child! She glanced at the clock. It was two hours since Mike had brought her back and still not three o'clock. There was plenty of time to go for a ride on Lilli Bell. She began peeling off her clothes quickly and then she reached inside the closet, changing into jeans, a shirt and tennis shoes. She had not yet obtained those boots which Mike had said she should have.

Dressed, she opened her door cautiously,

and very silently closed it behind her. On tiptoes, she crept down the hall. Maria was no longer in the family room. Darcy could hear her singing a Spanish song in the kitchen.

Holding her breath, she slid open the patio glass door and stepped outside. She did not want Maria to see her go — not that there was anything wrong in letting the girl know she was merely going for a ride, but she was in no mood to talk to anyone just at the moment. If she did not get away from this house she would blow up!

With a quick glance around, and seeing no one, she dashed across the lawn, past the barn and corrals until she reached the stable.

Lilli Bell was there and Darcy quickly saddled her up. This was something Mike had taught her, little knowing what use she would make of it. Holding the reins tightly, she led the horse outside, mounted and struck off towards the west.

Once she reached the stretch of trees that shielded her from view by anyone on the ranch, she felt exhilarated. This was what she had needed — a chance to get away from the house, from the heavy pressures of her life. Not that this ride would do much towards a show of independence; it was not likely that Mike would return home before dark and she would be back long before then. No, it was merely the knowledge that at least she was not sitting there brooding, *obeying* him about staying put, that lifted her spirits, even if he never knew about it.

She laughed at herself, and it felt good. There had been too many tears lately, too. She reached the spot by the creek where Mike had brought her that day. Impulsively, she dismounted and tied Lilli Bell to a tree. While the horse grazed placidly, Darcy wandered over to the water's edge and dropped down on her knees.

The water was looking clearer today, bluer, not quite so brackish as it had been before. A large old live oak on the other side of the bank cast inky blue shadows on the slow-moving water. She could hear the chirping of sparrows in the tree above the restless flow of the water.

It was so peaceful here, so timeless. It seemed to make personal problems fade into insignificance. Nature went her steady way, season by season, without paying the slightest heed to man's — or woman's turmoils and concerns. This stream, an offspring from a river miles away to the north, must have been here long before she was born and it would still be flowing when she died. Darcy wondered fleetingly if Mike's mother had come here, as she had, for peace and serenity, for a healing of one's soul.

After a long while, Lilli Bell's neighing roused her. She stood up, brushed her jeans off and stretched. "Shall we ride farther?" she asked the horse as she untied the reins and mounted.

She was not ready to head back to the ranch just yet. She was reluctant to shed all this peaceful quietness. Out here one could almost imagine oneself all alone in the world — without problems, hurts, heartaches.

She decided to follow the creek for a distance, so she headed an obliging Lilli Bell in a north-westerly direction.

There was much to see. Once she spotted a jack rabbit scurrying beneath a bush. She saw quails, a redbird, a grackle on a tree limb making its funny whirling noise, and a pair of squirrels prancing playfully across a clearing. The hum of insects rose from amidst tall weeds.

The creek curved and twisted tortuously. Several times she lost sight of it as she had to make another trail because of gnarled tree roots or cactus or tall weeds. As she tried to skirt Lilli Bell around a thick patch of thorny mesquite, she was suddenly aware that the sun was no longer blazing overhead, that it had been quite a while since she had felt its intense rays on her skin. She looked up and saw thick grey clouds building up. The air was cooler, too, so it must be much later than she had imagined.

She drew Lilli Bell to a halt, and sat very still listening. She had not seen the creek for some time she realised, straining her ears, but no sound of tinkling thrusting water came to her.

She looked about anxiously. The land rose and dipped here. This area was thick with mesquite and underbrush. She had meandered erratically, never giving her course a thought. If she had considered at all subconsciously, it had been with the idea of following the creek back to the ranch in the same way she had come, but she had now lost the creek and the clouds had completely blocked out the sun. She was, she realised, quite simply lost.

She turned the horse around and headed back in the direction she had come, hoping that she would find the creek. By now, she was not only growing uneasy, but tired as well. She gazed about intently. Mesquites, tall weeds, a cottonwood tree lay ahead. She could not remember seeing any of this before in this exact arrangement, and realised she must be going in the wrong direction.

A fine mist began to fall, adding to her general misery and discomfort. If it started to rain, things were really going to be tough.

She fought back tears. She had brought this mess down on her own head, just for the sake of pride — of not wanting to give in to Mike's arrogant orders to 'stay put'. Misty wetness clung to her hair, fine droplets sprinkled her lashes, and penetrated gradually the thin shirt she wore. Poor Lilli Bell was beginning to look a bit damp around the edges, too. "I'm

251

sorry," Darcy murmured apologetically to the horse. "I know you must be tired, too, but we just *have* to keep on going."

She turned towards what she hoped was a more easterly direction. Clearly, she was wasting time attempting to relocate the creek. The ground became more rolling, and it was an uncomfortable ride — up and down, up and down — and she was becoming increasingly sore. But more than her own discomfort, Darcy felt concern for the horse. It had tramped miles and miles, and they still were nowhere near home as far as she could tell.

A rolling fog swept in, thick and white and terrifying, and almost at once Darcy was enveloped in a swirling, cloud-filled blanket. The horse stopped of its own accord and Darcy looked round in rising panic. She could scarcely see beyond the horse's head. This was much worse than she would have dreamed possible, for now she could not even see where she was.

Lilli Bell whinnied and Darcy patted her neck sympathetically. She took stock of her situation. Before the fog swept in, she was on a small rise. There had been thick, tall weeds standing on the left, a small clearing on the right and a clump of mesquite thicket just ahead. If she moved slowly towards the left as she went forward, maybe she would reach a clearing where she could see a bit farther ahead. Slowly they inched forward.

Almost immediately they were going down an incline. Looming up to the extreme left was a large, dark blob, which was probably mesquite. They inched right, zigzagging down the incline into a shallow valley.

They paused again and Darcy tried to get her bearings, trying to assess which way was to the east. The fog settled in still thicker. She felt as though she were in some nightmare fantasy. East — was it to the left or straight ahead? She chewed her lip worriedly.

It was growing greyer and now she had a new worry. It would soon be dark. But she had to keep going; she could not afford to waste a single moment sitting still. They progressed up another rise, and then slowly down another. Darcy knew that at this rate they were making hardly any progress at all, but she could not give up now. She *had* to find her way back. Once night fell, she would never have a chance.

She heard something crash through the undergrowth. It startled her and made Lilli Bell skittish. Darcy gripped the reins tightly in her hands. "Calm down," she said as soothingly as she could, despite her own quaking heart. "Calm down, Lilli Bell. It was probably only a rabbit."

The horse moved forward faster. They brushed against a mesquite. Its thorns tore at her bare arms and tall weeds licked at her legs. Darcy pulled on the reins as hard as she could. "Whoa! Lilli Bell! Whoa!" But the horse took her own head. They started up an incline, the horse jogging hard, Darcy struggling both to stay on and see ahead.

Suddenly a cottonwood grove loomed. Darcy tugged frantically on the reins, trying to steer the frightened horse to the right, away from the trees. And then a tree branch caught her unawares and her head banged into it with a jolt. She screamed as she fell from the horse.

Her head was throbbing, but what was worse was that Lilli Bell was now at the top of the rise and that she was galloping. "Lilli Bell! Come back!" Darcy yelled frantically. She struggled to her feet, tried to run, but buckled again to the damp earth, her ankle twisted, and Lilli Bell was gone, caught up and hidden in the swirling mist.

14

THE pain that streaked through her foot was excruciating and the wound on her head throbbed violently. Carefully she straightened out her leg and leaned in a half reclining position against the tree trunk. She closed her eyes and swallowed, willing the sick, faint feeling to go away.

After a long time she opened her eyes again. Her head still throbbed dully and, when she touched it, she could feel a bump, but her head had stopped swimming now, the violent sickness had passed. She peered through the mist at her outstretched foot. The ankle was swelling rapidly. Gently she reached down and slipped off the tennis shoe, which relieved some of the pressure.

Clearly she was going to walk nowhere. Wide-eyed with fear, she looked up at the darkening gloom. The fog was just as penetrating as ever and soon it would be completely dark, dark and thick with the swirling mist that seemed to have a life of its own. She would not have even so much as one friendly star to keep her company through the long night ahead.

She choked back the tears that threatened to spill over. She must think. Was there anything she could possibly do but sit here and wait? Would anybody have missed her at the house yet? Had Maria gone to her room and found her gone? Would Mike be likely to know of her absence yet? And would he check the stables, discover Lilli Bell gone as well, and realise Darcy had set out on a solitary ride?

Even if he did, he would have no idea which direction she had taken. Even if he had drawn all those logical conclusions, it could still be hours and hours before she was found. It might even be days! This was such a vast, lonely country, where men thought and dealt with acres and miles rather than tiny city blocks. And what would she do in the meantime, unable to walk, bound in by thickets and fog as she was?

There was the possibility that Mike would not even bother to search for her! She had already attempted to run away from him once today. He might decide to let her succeed this time! The thought was unbearable.

Tears did spill out this time, finally overcoming her completely with great, racking sobs. She had never felt so forlorn and frightened in her life, not even that day of her car accident. The accident had happened so fast, and she had mercifully blanked out, and when she had come to, briefly, Mike had been standing over her, then kneeling beside her to cover her with a black raincoat. And he had kissed her so very gently.

But gentleness from Mike was now a thing of the past. There had been none, in fact, since that day in the hospital, when she had wept because of her worry and concern over Kenny. Certainly there had been no gentleness in him today when he had found her in Vince's arms. Today there had been violence, until she had intervened — and afterwards, grim arrogance.

Darkness descended swiftly. Darcy huddled against the tree trunk, shivering. The night air was cool, although not really cold, but she was chilled to the bone now from the wetness. She rubbed her hands across goose-fleshed arms and peered upwards. There was no thinning in the dense fog, not even any occasional clear patches.

She squirmed on the hard ground, trying to curl up in a more comfortable position, but the movement jarred her ankle, sending sharp pain slashing through her foot again.

A coyote howled somewhere off in the distance, and Darcy shuddered. What if the horrid creature discovered her? She listened intently. The tall weeds and grasses rustled and swished around her and she imagined all sorts of life nearby, eyes peering at her, watching, waiting to pounce.

She knew she would have to get a grip on herself. It would be a long night and, if she let her imagination run wild, she would be a gibbering idiot by morning. Concentrating fiercely and determinedly, she forced herself to think of other things — anything that would while away the long, dark hours.

She shifted her position, and the movement brought a new twinge to her ankle. She was also suddenly aware that she was hungry. She had merely toyed with her food at lunch, in a fever of impatience to leave. At breakfast there had been the scene with Mike, and she had been too tense to eat more than a slice of toast. Now she felt hollow and shaky. The old adage came back to her: *Never set out on a solitary horseback ride without carrying a packed lunch,* she told herself with bitter humour. *Better yet, carry along a bedroll and pillow as well.*

She looked at the sky again. It was pitch dark above the swirling layers of fog. She wondered what time it was. It might be nine, midnight, two or three. She had lost all sense of time since she had first looked up to see grey clouds gathering. An eternity seemed to have passed since then.

Something crept up her bare arm, and with a shriek, she looked down, but it was only a caterpillar. She knocked it off and gasped with relief. She had had visions of a rattler; this country was crawling with them in the summer months. She looked nervously around her immediate vicinity, expecting to see one coiled up nearby, ready to strike.

She felt the beginnings of hysteria rising

again. She would have to do better than this — get her mind on something else at once.

She thought back to the day of her accident — the day Mike had pulled her away from a wreckage that had burst into flames only scant moments later. And he had knelt and kissed her ever so gently. It had been like the fluttering wing tip of a butterfly brushing against one's skin, so light, so fleeting, so elusive. Remembering all that had happened since, that kiss now seemed unbelievable.

Her body was stiff from the long horseback ride, the hours crouched on damp ground against a tree. Carefully, she pulled herself up into a standing position. Maybe if she moved very slowly . . .

She took two or three hobbling steps, but any strong pressure brought renewed pain to her ankle. It was hopeless. Tonight she wasn't going anywhere under her own steam — not even if she knew where to go.

She bit her lip, suffering with chagrin and self-contempt. Mike had called her a troublesome wife this afternoon. Well, she had certainly proved him right, even though it had been unintentional. She limped back to the tree and sank down again. How she longed for a hot bath and a soft bed! They were things she had always taken completely for granted in the past. She heard the howl of the coyote again, and the sound of another. They sounded closer. Dear God, she would go mad, sitting here, waiting, defenceless.

And then she heard something else. From a long distance away, muffled by the thick fog, she could hear the words, "Darcy! Darcy!"

Giddy, almost hysterically with relief, she jumped to her feet, forgetting the injured ankle until it began to give, and then she leaned against the tree, bracing herself with her hand. "Here! Oh, Mike, I'm here!"

"Peanut!" His voice was sharp now, penetrating the mist. "Where are you? Keep calling so I can find you!"

"Here. Mike, I'm here. Beside a tree!"

It seemed an eternity before he found her. She could hear his voice, knew he was getting closer, but though she strained her eyes, she could not see him.

But at last he came into sight. "Mike!"

She moved from the tree, stumbling towards him eagerly. He slid from the horse's back and in two strides had reached her. His arms clamped tightly around her, strong and secure and comforting. Yet he was cursing softly. "When Lilli Bell came back without you, I imagined you dead. Why were you so stupid as to go off on your own like that? Don't you realise the dangers in this country? I could beat you, Peanut! You're the most obstinate, hard-headed, troublesome . . . "

Darcy never heard the rest of the angry tirade as she fainted in his arms.

15

WHEN Darcy came to, she was on a horse, riding through cloudy fantasy-land. And she was cradled within a pair of strong arms.

Her head was fuzzy. Was this more imagination — after the long ordeal she had had? She turned her head slightly and met Mike's face close to her own. The night was so dark that even at this range she could barely see him, except for the whites of his eyes. But she could feel his warm breath against her hair. This was real! Mike was really here with her, holding her closely against his body.

"Mike?" she began tentatively.

"Don't talk," he growled. "We should be home soon. We'll talk after you've rested."

Darcy subsided meekly. She was too thoroughly exhausted to enter into an argument with him now, and by the sound of his voice, he was definitely angry.

Another half hour brought them to the

outskirts of the ranch. Darcy recognised a gate, the vague outline of one of the buildings. And the sky was lightening. It was still foggy and damp, but dawn was bursting forth above the cloud layers, giving a promise of glorious golden light later on.

Mike rode up to the house and dismounted, then reached up and gathered her into his arms. Felix came out of the back door just as Mike was about to enter, still with Darcy in his arms.

"*Dios*! You found her! I was just about to set out again when Maria said you hadn't returned."

"Yes. She was about five miles away, up to the northeastern section. Take care of the horse for me, Felix."

Felix nodded and Mike passed inside. Maria was in the kitchen, by the stove, and her eyes brightened when she saw them. "You've found her!" she said, just as Felix had. Then she crossed herself and looked heavenward. "I have been so worried."

"Fix her some hot soup, Maria," said Mike. "She must be starved, but she's too exhausted to eat anything heavy. Bring it to her room when you have it ready."

"*Si*," Maria agreed. "Right away."

Mike carried Darcy to her room, deposited her on the edge of the bed and said gruffly, "Get undressed. I'll run your bath water."

Despite her tiredness, she flushed as he stood looking at her. He cursed angrily. "You're my wife, Darcy, for God's sake! Do you really believe I intend to make advances to you *now*?" He turned abruptly towards the bathroom. "Better do as I say or I'll do it for you."

Fumbling, she did as he said, cringing in this ultimate embarrassment. But Mike didn't so much as look at her. He turned on the taps, shook some flakes of bubble bath into the water, then reached on the back of the bathroom door, took down her robe and flung it out to her.

Gratefully, she slid quickly into it and knotted the tie at the waist. He came back into the bedroom. "Now get into the tub. I'll be out here if you need me." When she looked up, surprised, he said harshly, "Can't have you falling asleep in the water."

She bathed quickly, longing to lie back and soak for hours in the relaxing warmth of the water. But she was conscious of Mike in her bedroom, waiting. If she took too long over her bath he was perfectly capable of coming in after her.

She was drying off with one of the thick terry towels when he knocked briefly on the door, opened it slightly and handed in one of her filmy, thin nightgowns. "Here," he said in a muffled voice. "I suppose you'll need this?"

"I . . . thank you," she stammered.

"Hurry up. Maria's brought your soup, and it's getting cold."

Darcy hurried. She dusted her body with perfumed dusting powder, slipped into the pale blue gown, and pulled on the robe over it.

She felt very self-conscious as she came out, flushed and faintly pink from her bath. The bed had been made down invitingly. Mike came to her, pulled off her robe and she slid into bed quickly, aware of the extreme thinness of the gown. But he appeared not to notice. "How's the ankle?" he asked as he brought the tray to her.

She leaned back against the mound of pillows and accepted the tray. "A little better, I think."

"After you've had a sleep, we'll take you into town and let Len check it."

"No," she said now. "It's only a sprain. I don't need a doctor, Mike."

"Not for that knot on your head, either?" He reached across the bed and touched her head gently where a lump penetrated beneath her hair.

"How . . . how did you know about that?"

He grinned. "When you fainted, I did a little examination." He watched her face flush and grinned even wider. "Now, don't go all Victorian again, Peanut. It was necessary. I had to find out if anything was broken and you were in no condition to tell me." His voice changed, the grin faded and he said briskly, "Now, eat up. After that you can get some rest."

"But Mike . . . " she stammered uncertainly, "I have to tell you . . . explain . . . "

He held a hand up. "I said it would keep. We'll talk later. Right now you need to rest."

The soup was delicious. It spread a lovely warmth through her and she drained the bowl to the last drop. Mike watched her keenly and, when she had finished, took the tray from her unresisting fingers. She

268

was already half asleep when he murmured softly, "Sweet dreams, Peanut."

Her room was engulfed in late afternoon shadows when she awoke. She yawned, and flipped over to look at the clock on the bedside table. It was five-fifteen and she had slept the entire day away!

She slid from the bed and hobbled to the window. Her ankle was still weak and painful, but not as it had been the night before. She looked out over the front lawn. The sky was still blazingly bright, but the live oak cast deep shadows across the walk and drive. Darcy watched two butterflies flitting around before she turned back to her room. It was time to get dressed. Suddenly nervous, she knew she would have to face Mike and his anger soon. This could not be put off indefinitely.

A light tap sounded on her bedroom door. She could not face Mike yet! She slid her arms hastily into her robe before calling out with extreme reluctance. "Come in."

Maria entered and stood smiling at her. "How do you feel now?"

"Almost as good as new," Darcy smiled. "I'm sorry I've been so much trouble for everyone."

"Don't think that," Maria scolded. "We are all very grateful to have you back unharmed. Last night must have been bad."

"Very bad," Darcy shuddered. "But I'm back now and I've wasted an entire day. I suppose I'd better get dressed."

Maria shook her head. "Mr Mike left orders. You are not to get out of bed at all today."

Darcy's eyes kindled. "Oh, he did, did he?"

"Yes, ma'am. I'm to bring you a tray for dinner."

"Nothing of the sort," Darcy exclaimed indignantly. "I've caused enough upsets already. I feel fine. I'll be up and dressed for dinner."

So Mike had ordered her to stay in bed, had he? Well, she would not! They would have to get something settled tonight about the business of her leaving and she needed all the confidence she could muster when she faced him. And lying in bed was not the way to get it. She intended to be fully dressed and away from this room before facing Mike.

She hobbled to the bathroom and took

another bath. This time she was able to soak in the warmth as she had wanted to do this morning. She stretched out luxuriously as the silky water lapped over her body and the heat penetrated her skin.

There was time also to shampoo and dry her hair. When she brushed it out it was a smooth, shining halo around her small face. She applied her make-up carefully and pulled a long lock of hair slightly over her forehead, making sure the bump just at the hair line was entirely covered.

While she dressed she heard Mike come in and go to his room, and all at once her hands shook nervously. What would she do if he still refused to let her go? she wondered wildly. Would she still have the courage to try to run away again? At the moment, she knew she had not. Yesterday had been so horrible.

She slipped on a white floor-length dress, with a swirling pleated skirt. She buckled a wide green belt at the waist and stood looking at her reflection. The dress was flattering to her, emphasising all the curves in the right places. *No* one *would ever know you'd spent the night*

in the wilds last night, she told herself
with a grim smile. But the dress needed
some sort of jewellery. She searched in her
jewellery box, but she didn't have anything
in the way of costume jewellery that would
enhance it. Both the pearls and the emerald
bracelet Mike had given her would have
been perfect, but she had returned them to
him, along with her rings. The dress would
have to hold its own without adornment.

She left the room and went slowly to the
family room, being careful of her ankle.
She sat down gratefully on the sofa and a
moment later Kenny came bouncing in.
He was bathed and dressed for bed and
he smelled sweet and clean as he came
and hugged her.

Mike came in at that moment and
stood looking down at her with a solemn
expression in his eyes. "How are you
feeling?" he asked politely.

"Fine," Darcy answered shyly.

"A drink?"

"Sherry, please." Maria came in and led
Kenny away to bed, promising him a story
if he came right away.

Darcy was left with Mike alone and all
at once she felt tongue-tied and awkward.

"Did — did you get any rest today yourself?" she asked as he handed her the drink.

"I slept a few hours this morning," he admitted. "The ankle all right?"

"Yes. It's still tender, but better than it was last night. I'm sure it will be as good as new in a few days."

Mike talked stiltedly about ranch matters as they waited for Maria to return from Kenny's room and serve dinner. Darcy felt as though they were two strangers talking and she wondered now whether she would have the courage to approach Mike about letting her leave.

The telephone rang in the study and Mike excused himself and went to answer it. A moment later she heard him say, "Oh, hello, Maxine," before, softly, he shut the door.

When he returned and they went in to dinner, Darcy's chin was stiff and unyielding. It was she who now spoke stiltedly and with an obvious effort.

They had coffee in the family room and, once Maria left them, Mike came and sat down beside her on the sofa. He lit a cigarette and took several puffs before he turned to her at last. His face seemed whiter tonight, somehow strained and tense; his dark eyes were shuttered and unreadable.

"So you want to leave," he said at last.

Darcy bit her lip and nodded. "Yes. Yes, Mike, I do."

He frowned and gazed at his cigarette. "I can understand your taking the car if you wanted to leave, but what did you expect to accomplish trying to get away by horse?"

"But I wasn't," she exclaimed. "I was only trying to . . . to blow some of the cobwebs away by taking a ride. I'd fully intended to be back long before dark." Her bottom lip trembled. "I'm sorry, Mike, I'm truly sorry for all the trouble I caused. I . . . I never meant to."

"And if you had succeeded in getting away in the car? Don't you think that would have caused a certain amount of trouble as well?"

She chewed her lip again. "Y-yes, I suppose so. But I well . . . "

"Well?" There was the sardonic lift to his eyebrows now as he looked at her intently.

The colour came and went in her cheeks.

"I felt I had to get away."

"You were going for good?"

She could not meet his gaze any longer. "Yes," she whispered.

"Why?"

Her eyelashes fluttered up and she looked at him in surprise. "Why? But surely you know!"

"Tell me." His voice was hard, a command.

She began awkwardly. "Because our — this marriage — it's all a big mistake."

"In other words, you want to get away from me, is that it?" Mike asked coldly.

She swallowed and nodded. "Y-yes." Her voice came out weakly, a mere thread.

Mike got to his feet, walked over to the glass patio door and stood looking out, his hands thrust deep into his pockets. "So you can marry Vince?" His voice was hard.

"No!" She got to her feet too, and limped slowly towards him. His back was to her, rigid and stony. He was so tall, so commanding. She felt dwarfed. "I told you both yesterday, I don't intend to marry anyone!" She choked out the words.

"Then it's just me you can't bear to be near." It was a statement, not a question.

"All right, then, go. You're free," he added in a harsh voice.

There was a note in his voice Darcy had never heard before. He almost sounded as though he were hurt. She touched his arm imploringly with her trembling hand. "Mike?" Her voice cracked a little. "Don't . . . don't you *want* me to go?"

He whirled around to face her. His face was dark, his jaw hard and inflexible. "Want you to go?" His voice was slightly unsteady. "Why should you imagine I want you to go?"

Her lips quivered as she gazed up at him in confusion. "But — you said you'd made a mistake — about me — about my being able to care for Kenny properly after he was so ill."

He gazed at her. "*I* said that? Never!"

Darcy stared at him in blank amazement. "Didn't you?"

His eyes were ablaze with something she couldn't define. There was anger and something else. "Of course I didn't!" he exclaimed. "I thought you were magnificent with Kenny. Who told you such a thing?"

"It — " She swallowed and shook her head. "It doesn't matter."

"Yes," he rasped, "it does matter. But we'll iron that out later." He grabbed her shoulders and pulled her up against him. "I've never wanted you to go, Peanut," he said huskily against her hair. "How could I when I love you so much?"

She drew back just a tiny fraction so that she could peer up into his face. "You — you — " She shook her head. "You can't possibly!"

He smiled suddenly, but it was a grim smile. "Oh, can't I?" His arms dropped from around her and she felt suddenly cold and bereft. "But you want to get away from me." He turned back to the window. "I'll drive you to town tomorrow myself. You won't have to run away from me again."

"But — " Her voice came out faintly. She gulped a breath of air and went on more strongly, aware now that his pride stood in the way. He had been hurt as badly as she. "But can I please change my mind and stay?"

He turned to look at her again. The light in his eyes was frighteningly intense. "Why?" he asked uncompromisingly.

"Because, you see," she struggled out,

hovering between laughter and tears, trying for the light touch, "I'm mercenary — I want my rings back, and the pearls and the bracelet." She laughed breathlessly. "I — I'll hug your neck if — if you'll give them back to me."

His arms came around her again, tight and strong so that she could scarcely breathe. "Say it," he whispered huskily. "Let me hear you say it."

Her face coloured slightly, but she said in a strong, firm voice, "Oh, Mike, I love you so very much!"

Neither of them said anything else for a long while. Mike kissed her eyes, her throat, her hair. There was a fiery intensity to his kiss as at last his lips claimed hers — their first shared kiss given without bitterness or anger or misunderstanding. Darcy's arms crept up around his neck and her fingers stole through his thick, dark hair. Her actions seemed to inflame him even more and he crushed her soft, warm, yielding body against the hard, passionate maleness of his.

At last they drew slightly apart, both smiling because they couldn't help it, and Mike lifted her up and carried her over to the sofa. Then, seated beside her and with his arms around her so that her head lay nestled against his chest, he said, "I fell in love with you the first time I saw you, Peanut, that day I pulled you away from the car. You were so pale that I was frightened you were going to die right there. And then you opened your eyes and looked up at me, and I thought you were the most beautiful creature I'd ever seen."

"And — you kissed me," she said shyly, certain now that it had been no hallucination.

He nodded and lifted one of her hands up and kissed her palm. "Yes. I couldn't seem to stop myself."

"And you stayed with me at the hospital all that time when I was unconscious."

"I remember that they didn't like it much at first," he smiled. "After all, I wasn't 'family'. But as I refused to budge until they came up with some 'family' to take my place there wasn't much they could do about it." There was a curious ring in his voice. "I was afraid if I left, you would die and go away from me for ever. Somehow I felt if I stayed there, *willing* you to live, you would for me!"

"Oh, Mike!" Darcy all but wailed. "If only I'd known! All these months we wasted!"

He lifted her chin up and kissed her lips again. "When did you first know you loved me, darling?"

"I think," she said unsteadily, "that I loved you from the first, too. For a long time I thought I'd dreamed that — about your kissing me after the accident. I couldn't get you out of my mind. But I really knew for sure the day I went shopping with Maxine. Maxine said — well, she said a lot of things. Anyway," she ended flatly, "I thought you loved her and had quarrelled and that you'd married me while you were still angry with her. I thought you wanted her back again."

"Were you jealous?"

She wrinkled her nose at him. "Horribly!"

"But there was never anything between us, darling. For years people around here just sort of paired us off, but I never had any intention of marrying Maxine. She might have wanted to, but I never did. I never wanted to marry at all until I met you."

Darcy decided to keep silent for ever about just exactly what Maxine had said.

After all, there was no point in raking all that over the coals any more. But one thing she did have to ask. "But, Mike, I saw you kissing her the other day and . . . "

"You saw her kissing me," he corrected. "And I can tell you she won't be doing it again."

"Mike, that night — when I refused the bracelet and you didn't come home — Did you — I thought — " She trailed off, still miserable at the memory.

He smiled. "You thought I was with Maxine?"

She nodded.

He laughed and bent to kiss the tip of her nose. "I'll admit that's what I hoped you'd think. But the truth is I drove around on my own half the night."

She squeezed his hand. "Oh, Mike, I'm so sorry." She was silent for a moment, then asked, "But — if you knew you loved me, why did you tell Vince to invite me to his house the next day?"

He looked at her quickly. "I thought you were interested in him. And it seemed obvious you had no use for me or my gifts, either! I guess I was trying to be fair to you — let you have a chance to be with him."

"Yet when you found me in his arms beside the car yesterday you looked ready to commit murder!"

"I was ready to do murder! All my noble, generous intentions to let you go to him went by the board, Peanut!"

Darcy was silent. There was one thing she would still like to know. He squeezed her hand. "What's still bothering you, darling?"

"Maxine. She called you tonight before dinner."

He tugged on a strand of her hair. "What big ears you have, my dear," he said. "She was only calling to say goodbye. She's going out to California to visit friends for a few months." He pulled her closer against him and said, "And that's enough of that nonsense. I've got more important things to discuss."

"Like?"

"I had a letter from Don yesterday. With all this turmoil I forgot to tell you. He's remarried and he and his new wife will be flying home and taking Kenny back with them. They'll be here next Monday."

"Oh!" Darcy gasped in dismay. "I'll miss Kenny so much, though!"

He smiled. "Ever thought of starting a family of your own, Mrs Trent?" She flushed scarlet and he bent and kissed her lips gently. "You're adorable, you know that? Now, where were we? Oh, yes. I was just about to ask your preference for our honeymoon. Where would you like to go?"

"Honeymoon?"

"Yes, my sweet, honeymoon. As soon as Don and his wife come and go, we'll be leaving ourselves for a few weeks. So where shall we go?"

"It doesn't matter," she said softly. "As long as I'm with you."

He kissed her again, longingly. It was a kiss that left Darcy shaken by the depths of her desire. "I never intended our marriage to be temporary, you know," he told her now, softly. "But it seemed the only way to get you to marry me at once. I thought I would have plenty of time to win you later. But every time I approached you, you turned on me like a wildcat."

"But that," she flushed again, then went on bravely, "was because I thought you only wanted to make love to me without loving me. I had to fight myself to hold back."

His eyes blazed. "And now," he said gently, but with a teasing gleam in his eyes, "will you be willing to share my king-sized bed?"

Her face was only faintly pink as she met his eyes boldly. "For the rest of my life," she promised.

He buried his face in her silvery cloud of hair and murmured exultantly, "You're mine now, Peanut. Really mine. For ever."

She would not quarrel with him about that.

Other titles in the
Ulverscroft Large Print Series:

TO FIGHT THE WILD
Rod Ansell and Rachel Percy

Lost in uncharted Australian bush, Rod Ansell survived by hunting and trapping wild animals, improvising shelter and using all the bushman's skills he knew.

COROMANDEL
Pat Barr

India in the 1830s is a hot, uncomfortable place, where the East India Company still rules. Amelia and her new husband find themselves caught up in the animosities which seethe between the old order and the new.

THE SMALL PARTY
Lillian Beckwith

A frightening journey to safety begins for Ruth and her small party as their island is caught up in the dangers of armed insurrection.

THE TWILIGHT MAN
Frank Gruber

Jim Rand lives alone in the California desert awaiting death. Into his hermit existence comes a teenage girl who blows both his past and his brief future wide open.

DOG IN THE DARK
Gerald Hammond

Jim Cunningham breeds and trains gun dogs, and his antagonism towards the devotees of show spaniels earns him many enemies. So when one of them is found murdered, the police are on his doorstep within hours.

THE RED KNIGHT
Geoffrey Moxon

When he finds himself a pawn on the chessboard of international espionage with his family in constant danger, Guy Trent becomes embroiled in moves and countermoves which may mean life or death for Western scientists.

TIGER TIGER
Frank Ryan

A young man involved in drugs is found murdered. This is the first event which will draw Detective Inspector Sandy Woodings into a whirlpool of murder and deceit.

CAROLINE MINUSCULE
Andrew Taylor

Caroline Minuscule, a medieval script, is the first clue to the whereabouts of a cache of diamonds. The search becomes a deadly kind of fairy story in which several murders have an other-worldly quality.

LONG CHAIN OF DEATH
Sarah Wolf

During the Second World War four American teenagers from the same town join the Army together. Forty-two years later, the son of one of the soldiers realises that someone is systematically wiping out the families of the four men.

THE LISTERDALE MYSTERY
Agatha Christie

Twelve short stories ranging from the light-hearted to the macabre, diverse mysteries ingeniously and plausibly contrived and convincingly unravelled.

TO BE LOVED
Lynne Collins

Andrew married the woman he had always loved despite the knowledge that Sarah married him for reasons of her own. So much heartache could have been avoided if only he had known how vital it was to be loved.

ACCUSED NURSE
Jane Converse

Paula found herself accused of a crime which could cost her her job, her nurse's reputation, and even the man she loved, unless the truth came to light.

MORNING IS BREAKING
Lesley Denny

The growing frenzy of war catapults Diane Clements into a clandestine marriage and separation with a German refugee.

LAST BUS TO WOODSTOCK
Colin Dexter

A girl's body is discovered huddled in the courtyard of a Woodstock pub, and Detective Chief Inspector Morse and Sergeant Lewis are hunting a rapist and a murderer.

THE STUBBORN TIDE
Anne Durham

Everyone advised Carol not to grieve so excessively over her cousin's death. She might have followed their advice if the man she loved thought that way about her, but another girl came first in his affections.

A GREAT DELIVERANCE
Elizabeth George

Into the web of old houses and secrets of Keldale Valley comes Scotland Yard Inspector Thomas Lynley and his assistant to solve a particularly savage murder.

'E' IS FOR EVIDENCE
Sue Grafton

Kinsey Millhone was bogged down on a warehouse fire claim. It came as something of a shock when she was accused of being on the take. She'd been set up. Now she had a new client — herself.

A FAMILY OUTING IN AFRICA
Charles Hampton and Janie Hampton

A tale of a young family's journey through Central Africa by bus, train, river boat, lorry, wooden bicyle and foot.

DEATH TRAIN
Robert Byrne

The tale of a freight train out of control and leaking a paralytic nerve gas that turns America's West into a scene of chemical catastrophe in which whole towns are rendered helpless.

THE ADVENTURE
OF THE
CHRISTMAS PUDDING
Agatha Christie

In the introduction to this short story collection the author wrote "This book of Christmas fare may be described as 'The Chef's Selection'. I am the Chef!"

RETURN TO BALANDRA
Grace Driver

Returning to her Caribbean island home, Suzanne looks forward to being with her parents again, but most of all she longs to see Wim van Branden, a coffee planter she has known all her life.

DEAD SPIT
Janet Edmonds

Government vet Linus Rintoul attempts to solve a mystery which plunges him into the esoteric world of pedigree dogs, murder and terrorism, and Crufts Dog Show proves to be far more exciting than he had bargained for . . .

A BARROW IN THE BROADWAY
Pamela Evans

Adopted by the Gordillo family, Rosie Goodson watched their business grow from a street barrow to a chain of supermarkets. But passion, bitterness and her unhappy marriage aliented her from them.

THE GOLD AND THE DROSS
Eleanor Farnes

Lorna found it hard to make ends meet for herself and her mother and then by chance she met two men — one a famous author and one a rich banker. But could she really expect to be happy with either man?

PREJUDICED WITNESS
Dilys Gater

Fleur Rowley finds when she leaves London for her 'author's retreat' in the wilds of North Wales that she is drawn, in spite of herself, into an old tragedy.

GENTLE TYRANT
Lucy Gillen

Working as Ross McAdam's secretary, Laura couldn't imagine why his bitchy ex-wife should see her as a rival.

DEAR CAPRICE
Juliet Gray

Clifford Fortune married Caprice but his brother, Luke, knew the marriage was a mistake. He could allow himself to love Caprice blindly but that would be betraying his own brother.

LEAVE IT TO THE HANGMAN
Bill Knox

Dope, dynamite, guns, currency — whatever it was John Kilburn and his son Pat had known how to get it in or out of England, if the price was right. But their luck changed when one of them killed a cop.

A VIOLENT END
Emma Page

To Chief Inspector Kelsey there was no shortage of suspects when Karen Boland was murdered, and that was before he discovered that she stood to inherit substantially at twenty-one.

SILENCE IN HANOVER CLOSE
Anne Perry

In 1884 Robert York is found brutally murdered at his home in Hanover Close. When, three years later, Inspector Pitt is asked to investigate, the murder remains unsolved.

THE SONG OF THE PINES
Christina Green

Taken to a Greek island as substitute for David Nicholas's secretary, Annie quickly falls prey to the island's charms and to the charms of both Marcus, the Greek, and David himself.

GOODBYE DOCTOR GARLAND
Marjorie Harte

The story of a woman doctor who gave too much to her profession and almost lost her personal happiness.

DIGBY
Pamela Hill

Welcomed at courts throughout Europe, Kenelm Digby was the particular favourite of the Queen of France, who wanted him to be her lover, but the beautiful Venetia was the mainspring of his life.

SKINWALKERS
Tony Hillerman

The peace of the land between the sacred mountains is shattered by three murders. Is a 'skinwalker', one who has rejected the harmony of the Navajo way, the murderer?

A PARTICULAR PLACE
Mary Hocking

How is Michael Hoath, newly arrived vicar of St. Hilary's, to meet the demands of his flock and his strained marriage? Further complications follow when he falls hopelessly in love with a married parishioner.

A MATTER OF MISCHIEF
Evelyn Hood

A saga of the weaving folk in 18th century Scotland. Physician Gavin Knox was desperately seeking a cure for the pox that ravaged the slums of Glasgow and Paisley, but his adored wife, Margaret, stood in the way.